CW00433666

First print edition: June 2018

ISBN-13: 978-1722147075
ISBN-10: 1722147075

Crime

and

Cremation

Diny van Kleeff

The End

-- Louella's Blog: A Passion for Crime --

Imagine clambering out of your foamy, lavender-scented, bath-water and hugging a soft towelling robe around your damp limbs before sliding a radiator-warmed, over-sized t-shirt onto your still hot skin, then padding bare-foot to sit on the edge of your sumptuous, pillow-strewn bed. Imagine slathering lemon-mouse scented cream over your feet and painstakingly massaging it into the full length of each leg, before sliding your lemony legs under deliciously cool, cotton covers.

Imagine performing your bedtime routine, the one you do on every ordinary night, knowing that underneath your bed is a man who slithers in there while you are soaking away the day, who probably peeks through the hole in the bathroom door where the door-knob fell off a few weeks ago, who sees your skin glistening wet and probably watches as you soap yourself down.

Imagine, knowing the small bump in your bed, that wasn't there three days ago is probably his hard-on as he revels in the flesh he has seen and the act he is undoubtedly anticipating.

Imagine having to pretend you have no idea he is there, because the only way to stop him is to catch him…

-- End of blog post --

18th September

Hey Emily, look I'm suddenly getting hundreds of LIKES on that very first blog post I wrote at the beginning of the summer," shrieks Louella.

"Bloody hell Louella, that's impressive!" I admit, "But, I'm still not convinced I'll ever get used to being in a character in your erotic fantasy!"

Louella smirks, "Have you seen how many new people are following me this week!"

"I've read every one of your posts, at least four times now," says Harry

I cover my face with my hands, "It's just so embarrassing."

"You'll get a share of the advertising revenue," says Louella, as if that makes it totally fine.

I shrug my shoulders in defeat, "Are you sure no-one can trace any of what you write back to us."

"You know I'm careful," moans Louella, "hey, I've even thought of a title for the book – and the film, when it gets optioned."

I shake my head in mock horror, "Oh Louella, you really are going to make a great author one day - so long as you don't expect me to keep being your muse!"

"Well, that entirely depends on what you intend to do with your life," says Louella.

Harry peers at me with a wicked expression, "Perhaps you and Mr Creepy could team up after you finish university."

I fake a shudder of disgust while tightly crossing my fingers behind my back, "This summer was a one off – none, I repeat, NONE of it, will ever happen again."

The Associates

20th June

The postman strolls up to our front door at the exact moment I stumble out of it, lugging my mum's hideous, 1970s, floral suitcase. I have grabbed my teenage prerogative to remain at home while my parents and younger sister visit relatives in the Cornwall, thus avoiding snooty Aunt June with her highly academic, extremely creepy, third husband and their even weirder (and decidedly unattractive), adopted sons.

I notice the postie appreciate my new super-short, shorts with a prolonged glance, for which I reward him with a nonchalant drop and over-extended retrieval of the letters he nervously stuffs into my hands, his face reddens but his bright-blue eyes do not avert. He is tall, blonde and bookishly-handsome.

I coyly tuck a newly highlighted strand of hair behind my ear, give him my sweetest smile and watch him saunter self-consciously back down the drive. The grimy curtains of the empty house opposite twitch, I guess someone has finally moved in there.

Dad clocks my innocent flirting and I spot him have a few curt words with Mum, who then drags me inside for a repeat of 'The Talk'. I duly acknowledge the gravity of my inappropriate behaviour with as much faked sincerity as my eighteen years can muster. Satisfied with my duplicitous performance, I wave them off then prance inside like an unleashed puppy to do, well, whatever I want to do.

Unfortunately, in a moment of euphoric, post-A level madness and with aggressive encouragement from my militant feminist tutor, I signed up for a summer correspondence course on feminist politics. It really did seem like a good idea at the time and something that would be a great introduction to my degree course; however, it's only the third day of my summer break and already I regret being tied down by a hugely inconsiderate minimum of three hours study per week, so I turn the music on louder than I would if my parents had been home and grab a bottle of Corona from Dad's stash at the back of the fridge, which is definitely off limits and settle into my home-alone, teenage rebellion, grade-A student style.

An hour later, bored to death of research, I stretch my arms above my head and do those eye exercises that you're supposed to do every twenty minutes when you sit in front of a computer. As I focus on the distance, which happens to be the living-room window of the house opposite, I spot our new neighbour staring back at me, only for a split second before he turns away from the window. I think nothing of it, until twenty minutes later (I set my phone to remind me – I intend to keep my twenty-twenty vision for as long as I can, unlike my bespectacled parents,) as I was saying, twenty minutes later, I do the same short-focus, long-focus exercise and see that once again I am being watched. Now, I haven't yet met this guy close-up and I have no idea if he is hot or not but, being a generous girl, I give him the benefit of the doubt and treat him to a full body, bust-stretch, side-on so even if he can't see the details, he'll get a nice silhouette. He pauses a moment longer than before then disappears. Feeling pleased with my neighbourliness, I finish up studying.

Louella arrives at eight o'clock with only the tiniest bag, which she swears contains her clothes for two weeks, although judging by the size, she must have only brought underwear. I guess she intends to live in my clothes for the duration - I know from experience that she has a bit of a thing for wearing other people's clothes.

We settle down on the sofa in our nightshirts, still wearing our trainers, which Mum hates, for a chic-flick fest. At about eleven-thirty, just as we both start to doze off, Louella hears a sound from the back of the house. The only light we have on, other than the television is a dim table lamp; the rest of the house is in complete darkness. A moment later I hear a noise from the kitchen, like a kind of soft scraping, probably the cat. Louella can be a bit of a drama queen and by the widening of her eyes and the teeth indented firmly in her lower lip, I can tell the noise is freaking her out. I get up to turn on the main lights and drag her into the kitchen so she can see for herself that it is nothing to worry about, but the lights won't switch on, so I guess they must be on a different circuit to the plug-in lamp. There is nothing for it but to flick the fuse in the garage.

"Please don't go into the garage in the dark," begs Louella, looking like the next victim in a teen-slasher-movie.

"Its fine, the fuse is always blowing, it happened like, three times in the past week," I lie.

Then we both hear the noise, but this time it is coming from my dad's study. Bloody cat! I grab one of Mum's candles, the one she thinks is far too pretty to use and casually light it.

"Come on," I grasp Louella's hand – not because I'm scared but, if I have to tramp all over the house by candle-light, then Louella can bloody-well come with me.

The study is a place where I am definitely not welcome and where Dad keeps his best bottle of whisky. The door is ajar, which it shouldn't be. I guess he left if open in his rush to get on the road, or the cat has learned to pull the door handle, either way, I need to extract the cat before it does any damage.

Louella stands about three feet behind me as I push the door the rest of the way open and wait for Charlton to saunter out. He is nowhere to be seen. The noise has stopped and I waft the candle around to try and get a better look; everything looks creepy in the inefficient, flickering light and I will admit to pulling a sharp intake of breath when I see that the window is about three inches open. That is definitely not something Dad would accidentally leave and he is the only one allowed in this room.

Louella grabs my hand with her sweaty one and squeezes it far too tight.

"Ow!"

"Sorry!" she whispers, "What do we do? There could be someone in the house."

I still don't want to believe that we have an intruder but, having watched enough horror movies, I am not going to take any unnecessary risks. Holding hands and white as sheets, we promptly exit the house and knock on the door of our next-door neighbour, whose husband happens to be a policeman.

PC Crink, Ed he says to call him, must be close to retirement – if his diet doesn't kill him before that. He follows us back to the house and flicks the fuse in the garage before checking the whole house. He spends longer than I deem necessary checking under my bed and in my wardrobe, then he closes and locks Dad's study window, declaring the house safe, secure and trespasser-free.

We wave him goodnight from our now brightly-lit house and double-lock the door behind him.

I am still convinced there is an innocent, non-evil intruder explanation for the noises and the open window. Louella is not and is on the verge of going back to the safety of her own home. I desperately point out that this is our first ever opportunity to spend a whole week completely parent-free and I for one, am not willing to give up on it. Reluctantly, she agrees, on the proviso that Harry comes over to stay with us.

Harry is nineteen, one year older than me and Louella but, our joint best-friend and we have hung together as a threesome for the last four years. In theory, it is a good suggestion to have a man in the house but, if my parents EVER found out, that would be the end of everything good I had ever known. Harry arrives by the back door, so that none of our nosey neighbours will spot him and rat on us.

On the second night, a loud knock on the front door makes us all jump. I send Harry upstairs with Louella to hide in my ensuite bathroom.

Ed's grin is lopsided and his breath smells sour with beer. He insists on coming in to check the doors and windows for us again, I try to put him off but the sneaky bastard has a cop's senses.

"What are you hiding, young lady? Have you got a boy hidden in there? I know what dirty little games you teens get up to when mummy and daddy are away."

I open the door wide in a gesture of innocence, "I'm sure the house is totally secure after your last check, but if you really think there is a possibility that we have missed something, then we would be eternally grateful for your help." I lay it on thick and notice he is leering at my sparkling cleavage. Louella and I had been experimenting with YouTube tutorials on cleavage enhancing techniques earlier this evening. Apparently they work.

Ed wanders around the house, making scant checks on the windows and doors, then heads upstairs. My heart is in my mouth as he enters my bedroom and instantly clocks the closed door of my bathroom.

"Who's in there?"

Fortunately, Louella heard Ed come in the house and hatched a failsafe plan. The door to the bathroom opens just a crack, with Louella revealing herself to be clad in only a towel, with a bath full of bubbly water steaming beside her.

"Hi PC Crink, I was just about to have a soak, is everything ok?"

Ed nods, "Just checking the house is safe and secure."

I can see the veins in his thick neck pulse heavily as he stands listening for a moment after Louella closes the bathroom door and noisily sploshes around in the bath. I feel sorry for Harry, hidden behind the door, having to watch as the girl he lusts after, who only sees him as a platonic friend, frolicking around in the bath in front of him.

Then Ed notices the missing door handle. Quick as a flash, I grab it off my shelf – another job Dad hasn't got round to doing yet. I shove it into the gaping hole, laughing, "Oops, that could have been embarrassing."

Ed looks over at my double bed, "So, where does your friend sleep?"

"In my sister's bedroom," I answered curtly, not liking where his mind is heading.

He shuffles over to the window and tests the locks, peering over at his own house, "Shit!" he mutters under his breath, then with a forced joviality, "Well now, everything seems secure. You ladies have a good night."

He stumbles back downstairs and slams the front door. I watch from the bedroom window as he gruffly greets his wife, who has just pulled up on the drive from work, an hour earlier than usual.

I knock on the bathroom door and go in. Louella is sat in the bath in her wet and now completely transparent underwear and Harry is stood in the corner hugging a towel to his groin, sweating profusely in the heat.

"This is a situation," I laugh.

Louella gets out of the bath and dries herself off in the bedroom, leaving Harry in the bathroom to sort himself out.

We are sat back on the sofa, pigging out on popcorn by the time Harry re-joins us.

"Well, we know for certain that he's a bit of a pervert," says Harry through a mouthful of popcorn, "maybe he's the one who tried to break in."

Louella does her cute, lip-biting thing again and Harry takes the opportunity to place his hand on her arm in comfort.

"I don't think it would be him, he's a cop, he may be getting a bit of a kick out of being our protector but I really doubt he'd risk his career to spy on us," I reason.

"So do you think there's ANOTHER perv' out there, trying to break in?" shrieks a hysterical looking Louella.

"NO, I still think it was the cat. I think Dad accidentally left his study window open and the cat escaped out of it before we managed to catch him."

"But you were scared too!" said Louella.

"Mostly because YOU were freaking me out," I point out.

Louella snuggles into Harry for comfort. I sit with my arms crossed defiantly until the end of the movie. However, my bravado disappears when I go to get a glass of water from the kitchen and realise the back door is ajar. It was definitely locked when Ed checked earlier.

We decide to sleep in the living room, in front of the television that night.

Harry leaves for work at his uncle's crematorium, sneaking out and narrowly avoiding our cute postie as he deposits his load with great deliberation in our letter-box, giving me just enough time to throw on a bikini top that matches perfectly with my tiny PJ shorts and nonchalantly open the curtains as he walks past.

His face flushes again and he continues to look back at me while crossing the road, then almost slams into the man opposite as makes his way up the scruffy path. The poor boy turns an even deeper shade of red when I see the man, who is definitely not cute, admonish him. Postie turns his concentration to the direction he is heading and I catch a wink from the neighbour as he unlocks a shabby, leaf-green Volvo and shoots off in a splutter of grey smoke.

"Urgh! Well, he's a potential perv'," I tell Louella.

"What, just 'cos he winked at you?" says Louella.

"It's the way he winked, and he's been spying on me," I argue.

Louella looks me up and down and I can feel one of her, 'I told you so' moments brewing.

"ALL men in the neighbourhood spy on you - especially when you go out wearing things like that."

"Fair point, but most of them aren't perverts," I counter.

"You mean most of them are better looking?" corrects Louella.

"Same thing."

"Well, let's just keep an eye on him and see if he comes near the house," says Louella.

We spend the day sunbathing in the garden and watch a marathon, eight episodes of the cosy, nineteen-eighty's detective series, 'Murder She Wrote', which gives me an excellent, if somewhat dangerous idea.

What if, I ask Louella and Harry that evening, there really is a pervert trying to get into our house? Chances are he has done it before and possibly worse. What if, like Jessica Fletcher, the author-detective in 'Murder She Wrote', we could lay a cunning trap and catch him. We'd be heroes and possibly even get a reward.

Harry looks interested when I mention the reward, but Louella just looked terrified, "Don't you think that's really dangerous?"

We talk through all the possible angles and eventually come up with a plan to find out if there really is a pervert stalking us, after all, as Harry so usefully points out; it could simply be a poltergeist opening the doors and making sounds. It takes a good twenty minutes and a large glass of Dad's SPECIAL whiskey to calm Louella down after that comment, which is a big mistake because Louella is at her most flirtatious when intoxicated. Poor Harry becomes visibly uncomfortable and has to make a discreet exit when Louella begins to describe how she would like to tie Harry Styles, of pop group 'One Direction', to the posts of my parent's four-poster bed and act out the rude parts of Fifty Shades with him – that could take a while, I haven't read it yet but, I believe there are quite a lot.

Anyway, back to the plan. We will retire to our bedrooms early that evening, leaving the kitchen window open just a crack. I will sleep in my own room and Harry will sleep in my bathroom.

We lay the broken door knob on the floor, as if it has fallen off again, so that Harry can peek through. Louella is going to sleep in my parent's bedroom, with the door locked. We all have our phones at the ready; on silent, just in case.

A few minutes after midnight, I am woken by a noise; a creeping, scuffing, carpet rubbing sound coming from under my bed. I freeze, dead-still, barely breathing, wondering if Harry has slipped under the bed in an attempt to scare me. I peer into the darkness and see the bathroom door is firmly closed and my bedroom door is slightly ajar, which wasn't the case when I went to bed. I realise I need to pee, badly. Damn my nervous bladder! I cross my legs as tightly as I can, trying not make a noise. The scuffing sound continues under my bcd, ending with a whispered grunt. Paralysed with fear, I can't even reach under my pillow to text for help, then suddenly the perv' under my bed slips out and scurries down the stairs. I hear the kitchen door close and count to twenty, just to be sure.

I leap out of bed in a desperate dash to the bathroom, barely making it in time then remember, mid-flow, that the dark shape on the floor is Harry, who is now sitting up in his sleeping bag with a wide-eyed stare. Shit. He realises I have seen him and discretely turns away.

"Not a word Harry, not a WORD," I warn.

Recovering my dignity, I grab Harry's clammy hand and drag him to Louella in my parent's bedroom. I forget the door is locked and slam straight into it, god that hurts! Harry bangs on the door and Louella fumbles with the lock, taking an excruciating amount of time to open it. The bedside light is a comforting glow but the bed is a mess; strewn with pillows, towels, several pots of god-knows-what and Fifty-Shades propped open in the middle of it all. Louella kicks something under the bed and pushes the pillows back against the headboard.

"You alright Louella, you look flushed?" asks Harry.

I poke Harry hard in the ribs in indignation, "Excuse me, but I'm the one you should be asking if she's ok."

"Sorry, I uh, are you ok?"

"No, I bloody-well am not."

I clamber onto the bed, the shock of what has just occurred suddenly hitting me hard as I shakily slump into the mound of pillows. Harry and Louella squish either side of me with expectant stares. I take a deep breath and tell them what happened.

"Oh god, I'm so sorry," apologises Louella, "I didn't hear anything or I would have called the police."

"Hmm," I note, surveying the bed, "I guess you were otherwise engaged."

Harry looks at me quizzically. Sometimes I think he's a bit dim.

"So who was it under your bed, was it PC Crink, or the perv' from opposite?" asks Louella.

"Or the poor postman you tease every morning?" adds Harry, "Or someone else?"

"Who even says it has to be a man?" asks Louella but, we all agree a female pervert is highly unlikely.

Anyway, to cut a long story short, we come up with the perfect Scooby-Doo plan to catch him (or her), should they visit me again. In the morning, Harry cuts through the wooden legs at the foot of my bed, so the bed sits directly on the floor, then places them back under with a rope attached to each one; the idea being to pull the legs out, trap the perv' under the bed and call the police. Harry trails the ropes under the rug and into the wardrobe; he will sleep in my bathroom and leap out and yank the ropes if he hears anything. We test it a couple of times and the plan seems flawless.

Death by Bed

I am still ridiculously nervous about the whole thing but, never-the-less, agree that it is our duty to stop this pervert and potentially save future victims from terrible fates.

For the next few days, nothing happens, no intrusions, nothing but, on Wednesday, I have the funniest feeling that this will be the night, so I tell the others, which makes Louella incredibly anxious all day. It turns out that my intuition is spot on!

We wait until really late to go to bed, to reduce the chances of falling asleep on the job. Louella promises not to pick up her book, in case she gets lost in another fantasy and Harry has brought a gun from home. I freak out, but he explains that it's a replica and only shoots pellets. Louella says she thinks he looks hot with a gun - I've never seen Harry look so pleased.

At eleven fifty-seven we are in our places, wide-awake and ready.

At one-twenty I drop off to sleep, aided by the large glass of whiskey I self-administered before bed.

At two-thirty-six I wake with a jolt as my bed collapses. I assume it must be an accident, but then a torch-light blinds me and Harry pulls me off the bed.

He points the torch downward and I follow its beam then scream at the sight of the flabby, pale, limp arm poking out from under my broken bed. It isn't moving.

"Oh my god, oh my god," I grab onto Harry, who looks as bloodless as a cast member of 'Twilight'. Louella is stood in the doorway, doing a great impression of a goldfish.

"Has anyone called the police," I shakily enquire.

Evidently neither Louella nor Harry can speak as they both mutely shake their heads.

I gather my tattered nerves together and tentatively poke the arm with Harry's torch. Nothing. I push it and prod it, again, nothing. Then I whack it really, really hard with the torch but it doesn't even flinch.

"I think he must have passed out."

More mute nodding.

"Here, Harry, give me the ropes."

Harry looks at me, realising what is on my mind and starts to balk at the idea but, I grab the ropes from him and proceed to tie one end around the perv's wrist.

"Harry, Louella, you need to lift the bed, I'll truss him up while you hold the bed up then we can drag him out and call the police."

Louella remains in the doorway, not moving.

"Quickly, before he wakes up and gets himself out," I shriek.

That pushes her into action. I get ready with the ropes and also grab the baseball bat I keep next to the bed, incase he starts to stir. The bed rises slowly to reveal an unattractive man none of us recognise. He is solid, about fifty and wearing the kind of grubby tracksuit bottoms that only the most unfit men wear. His sneakers are in good condition but splattered with white paint and his t-shirt is probably from a supermarket. All-told not a fine specimen of a man.

I squeeze under the bed and tie his limp and surprisingly heavy arms together. Harry passes me the second rope and I wrap it round his legs all the way up to his thighs, threading the end of it through his arms and securing it with four knots. I step back to admire my handy-work, then take the end of the bed from Harry who, after a lot of over-exaggerated huffing and puffing, pulls the trussed-up body out from under it, where we can now survey him on my fluffy, pink rug.

"He looks like a pervert," observes Harry.

"Why can't they ever be cute?" I moan.

"And have good hygiene," adds Louella, wafting her hand around her head.

"I'll call the police," says Harry.

"Wait just a minute," I say, noticing a bump in his trousers. I kneel down to investigate and pull a thickly stuffed, cheap plastic wallet from his pocket. "Oh my god, there must be five hundred pounds in here!"

Harry grabs the wallet from me and pulls out a driving licence. Apparently our man is called Harvey J Goodlington and he lives just a couple of streets away. There are a couple of credit cards in the same name and two in the name of Asnat Fosnittar. Harry tips the rest of the wallet out onto the bed and another driving licence falls onto my covers in the name of Hans Gubner; it would appear that our perv' had more than one identity.

"I bet he's already wanted by the police," says Louella.

"Do you think we should keep the money, as a fee for catching him?" I suggest.

"Put twenty back, they'll be suspicious if there's nothing in it," says Harry.

"Oh, I had no idea you had such a criminal mind," gushes Louella.

I guess it's true that crime turns people on. A phone vibrates, making us a jump out of our skin.

"It's coming from underneath him, from his back pocket," Harry rolls him over to retrieve it.

"Answer it!"

Harry tries to pass the phone to me, "Don't be an idiot, I'm hardly going to sound like some fat bloke - you answer it."

Harry puts the phone to his ear and presses the button. He grunts a deep sounding 'Yeah' into the mouthpiece, which seems an adequate response to the person on the other end. Cleverly, Harry switches the speaker on and we all hear the gruff voice on the other end.

"Bud, you are in deep shit, Franko and Lena are blaming you for getting that bastard cop onto us, she reckons you got drunk and spilled too much info - reckon you aughta just get out of town. The boss wants your head – Hans, you hearing me?"

Harry grunts another deep affirmative.

"Okay buddy, I got a plan – gunna do you the biggest favour you ever been done in your sorry life, only 'cos I owe you – I'm gunna put my arse on the line and retrieve some of the cash so you can make a new start, Franko doesn't know there's cash in the haul, so I can swipe fifteen, he won't miss it. I'll leave it at Jackson's, under the booth at the end, pick it up when you get your coffee at half-ten – don't be late or some other lucky bastard will find it – you got that?" Harry grunted again, "and don't be early either, I can't afford to be seen with you," and the phone went dead.

"Wow Harry, class acting skills there," I compliment.

"Fifteen-thousand pounds," muses Louella.

The cogs in my brain start to whirr, "Fifteen-thousand pounds is a lot of money," I look at Louella and Harry.

"No way, don't even think about it," Harry looks horrified.

"We could do it, we just caught a real, live, potential killer – hell, we could be like a teen-crime fighting unit – Jessica Fletcher and the Scoobies."

"Which Scoobies? The ones from 'Scooby-doo' or the 'Buffy the Vampire Slayer' Scoobies?" asks Louella, "cos if there's a choice between Buffy and Daphne, I'd rather be Buffy."

"I think I'd rather be Shaggy than Xander, although I'm not sure there's much difference, other than the dog," adds Harry.

"I'm serious."

"Oh my god," groans Louella, staring down at our flabby perv', "I think he's stopped breathing."

Harry and I kneel down and try to see if his chest is moving, then Harry grabs the guy's wrist and feels for a pulse, he shakes his head, "He's a gonner."

We all sit back for a moment, not sure what to do.

"Tea," I suggest. My mother always says important decisions should be made over a pot of tea, so we head down to the kitchen and make a one.

Louella is shaking and Harry is looking perplexed. I'm actually feeling rather hyped – after all, we just took down a dangerous criminal and now we are going to cash in on the mother-lode.

"Shouldn't we phone the police?" asks Louella.

"I guess so," agrees Harry.

My mind is whirring with ideas and a niggling worry that we may actually get in trouble for killing the bloke, even though it wasn't our intention. I have an idea, "Do you think they'll accuse us of murdering him?" I tentatively suggest.

Louella's face drains of all blood and her mouth does the goldfish thing again. Harry takes advantage of her vulnerability and slings his arm around her shoulders, "It was an accident - we only meant to capture him."

"So man-slaughter then?"

"Shit no, Em," descries Harry.

"It's possible," I counter, "after all; we did set a trap that we should have known had the potential to cause serious injury or death."

"But they couldn't blame us, could they?" Louella whispers.

"I think they could, don't you Harry?"

He shrugs nonchalantly but his downcast eyes answer 'yes'.

"Oh Em! What do we do?" cries Louella.

"Harry can get rid of a body – can't you?" I stare pointedly at the poor lad.

It takes him a moment to catch on, "No way… my uncle would never allow it."

"But you know how to work a cremator?"

He nods.

"And you could borrow one of the vans?"

He nods again.

"Tonight."

"Now?"

"Yes," I fold my arms and try to look like I mean business, "you can sneak one of your uncle's vans, collect the body, take it to the crematorium and toast it before anyone realises he's missing, then tomorrow, we go to the café and collect the cash. It's a perfect plan."

Harry looks at Louella and I can actually see the cogs in their brains trying to assimilate my words.

"Fifteen grand is a lot of money and we would be doing the world a favour by getting rid of this scumbag," says Harry.

"Do you really think we could get away with it," asks Louella, her eyes wide and Bambi-ish.

I nod confidently.

Harry nods back. Thirty minutes later he arrives at the house with one of his uncle's vans and just before dawn cranks up the daylight, we heave the body into it. Two hours later, the evidence is a pile of ash and we are back in my living room. Harry has to be back at the crematorium in two hours and the money needs to be collected in four, so we simply sit and stare glaze-eyed at the news channel until one-by-one, we doze off.

Harry wakes with a start as his phone rings in his pocket, "Shit! It's my uncle."

He answers the phone and gets it in the neck for being late.

"Did he notice anything suspicious?" I ask.

"He didn't say anything, he's just pissed because we've got four cremations to do today and he needs me there ASAP," says Harry.

"Well we'd better work out where Jacksons is," says Louella, looking relieved.

Thank goodness for Google, a few clicks and Louella and I locate the only café named Jacksons in the vicinity and fortunately, it's within walking distance. We set off with time to spare, arriving fifteen minutes before the pick-up is due. Louella is increasingly warming to our newfound criminality and actually offers to go in and collect the package while I stand guard outside. It's a surprisingly busy place, filled with a spectrum of the local population. Louella reappears after five minutes carrying two cups and a significant weight in her previously empty back-pack.

We sit on a bench outside, drinking our teas and pretending very hard to be the nonchalant teens we normally are, which is difficult when you are mid-heist. I leave half my tea un-drunk because I can feel my bladder starting to panic again and my nonchalance is beginning to wane. We head back home and sleep until four o'clock in the afternoon when we are abruptly woken by the sound of the doorbell.

"Oh my god, it's the police!" shrieks Louella.

"Really?"

"I don't know, but it might be," she wails.

I peek through the spyhole.

"It's just a couple of kids," I reassure her as I lift the locks and open the door.

I vaguely recognise the girls from the neighbourhood, they are about seven and nine years old and inform me they are selling boxes of cookies to raise money for charity. We buy two boxes and settle down to munch through the lot when I notice a note taped to the inside of the lid of each of the boxes.

Thank you for buying our delicious cookies, we are raising money for our little brother Aiden. He has a rare type of cancer and the only treatment that can cure him is in the USA and costs over two-hundred thousand pounds. Your purchase and any further contributions are gratefully received.

Carly, Christina and Aiden's Mummy and Daddy xxx

There is a website address where further donations can be made. I look at Louella and she looks quizzically back at me.

"Don't you see?" I ask.

"See what?"

I'm feeling kind of Zen now, "We could donate the stolen money to help little Aiden get better."

"Kind of like Robin Hood, only taking from the bad instead of the rich and giving to the sick instead of the poor?"

Louella is getting the idea.

"And what if we were to catch more bad guys, and get more money? We could raise the whole amount and save Aiden's life – we'd be heroes!"

We talk the idea over with Harry when he gets back. It takes a lot of feminine persuasion, aided by our YouTube tutorial enhanced cleavages and some whiskey-fuelled flirting by Louella to bring him on board with the plan.

"So how the hell are we going to find more bad guys with stashes of cash?" he asks.

"Do we really have to kill them?" asks Louella.

I shrug my shoulders, the excitement and stress of the last twenty-four hours are catching up with me and I am too tired to think, "Let's discuss the details tomorrow, right now I need to sleep."

Fifty-Shakes of Milk

-- Louella's Blog: A Passion for Crime --

Fuelled by the adrenalin of their first kill and the musky scent of the stacked hundred-dollar bills piled before them, the three friends found themselves inexplicably aroused and in desperate need of a release from the heady tension that was stopping them from being able to fall asleep.

It was Angela who broke first, after gulping half a tumbler of whiskey she felt her inhibitions melt away and silently took Andrew's hand and placed on her lap. He glanced at her, uncertain for only a moment before he saw the pleading in her eyes. Sasha watched hungrily from behind a cushion...

-- End of blog post --

"Seriously! NO!" my cheeks burn harshly, "I'm not sure I can even look at you and Harry after reading that!"

"It's not us," said Louella.

"It's based on us," I counter.

"Just look at the number of hits we've had."

It is an impressive number.

"I've got people paying for adverts on my blog now," Louella points to a column of dubious boxes proclaiming 'BEST ORGASM EVER' and 'Be the DUDE she dreams of, not the DUD she married'.

"Nice," my sarcasm is undisguised.

"I don't see how you can get all uppity about a teeny bit of erotica when your CV features murder and theft? You kind of leapt over a big moral boundary with that, so come down off your high-horse and give me some literary appreciation, please."

"So is this who we are now – sex-mad, looting killers?"

"Two out of the three," mutters Harry, looking pointedly at Louella.

"No! No we are not," but I secretly wonder if maybe we are heading that way. "By the way, you really are a talented writer."

Louella actually blushes, which is surprising, considering the stuff in her head, "What I really want is for a publisher to pick it up and turn my blog into a novel - that really would earn us some good money."

"Yeah, well, you never know. I'll try really hard to pretend it isn't me featuring in your fantasies," I concede.

It's Saturday, over three weeks since The Bed Incident. The cash is stashed in my wardrobe, tucked behind my all-seeing prom dress. My parents returned from their trip a week ago and everything feels like normal. Harry glued the legs of my bed back together and we topped Dad's whiskey bottle up with a cheap whiskey Harry borrowed from his parent's house.

"Emily," my sister Francis is yelling.

"What?"

"That postman you fancy is loitering on the driveway."

God, I'm going to kill her. I look out of my bedroom window and there he is, pretending to sort through his bag, "How do I look?"

Harry looks me up and down, "Hot."

"Hot as in sweaty or hot as in attractive?"

"Both."

"Just get down there, he's not going to care what you're wearing," says Louella.

I give my hair a quick pat-down and leap down the stairs, then slow down and casually saunter out to collect the post.

"Oh, hi there, I didn't realise you were still out here," I lie.

"Oh, er… hi," he's gone bright-red again.

I glance up from the letter I am diligently staring at, making my eyes as wide as I can, which is never as Bambi-ish as Louella, "So, do you work every day?"

"I'm trying to pay my way through university and this job works around my classes," then he adds, "I'm free every afternoon until I start back in September though," he looks pointedly at me.

I gulp a deep breath of air and take the plunge, "I was thinking going to the cinema this afternoon, if you fancy joining me?"

"That would be great, shall I pick you up at two – I've got a car," he says.

Score me! The dude has a car.

"Name's Malcolm, by the way," he reaches out his hand to formally shake mine.

"Emily, but you can call me Em – do you go by Mal?"

"Malcolm."

Great, a hot date with his own car, I can live with the old guy name. I wave him off, noticing, as I turn, that the creepy guy from opposite is standing stock-still at his side gate, watching me. I run back into the house and announce my success to Harry and Louella. Harry is on his way out, his uncle called him in to work for the afternoon.

The film is terrible, which is great because Malcolm pays more attention to me than the screen. He's a great kisser and respectful with his hands, which I can deal with – contrary to what my friends believe, I don't always want to give it all up on the first date. We blink our way out of the dark cinema into the bright, late-afternoon sun and head down the street to grab a burger. We chat and flirt and I learn that Malcolm is studying to be an engineer and dreams of building gravity-defying bridges when he graduates. He tells me about his family; an older sister who works in France and his mum, who has just lost her job at Patcham and Co and is relying on his meagre wage to keep them afloat until she finds another job. I feign interest in his family and ask how his mum lost her job. Apparently, she was sacked for losing a contract but, the real truth is that she wouldn't sleep with her sleazy boss and he got pissed and gave her the boot. Now that really does spark my interest.

"So, what's the name of this sleaze-ball boss?" I enquire.

"Why do you want to know his name?" Malcolm asks.

Good point, I need to play it cool - this guy could be our next client and I can't afford to raise any suspicion.

"Oh, it's just that my mum's friend Janice used to work for Patcham and Co a few years back and she left after some sort of nasty incident with her boss, I don't know the details because I only overheard her and my mum talking about it."

"Do you know her boss's name?"

I pluck a name from the air, "I think it was something like Jameson?"

"Must have been a different guy, my mum's boss was Denton – sounds like the whole company is full of arseholes!"

Malcolm drops me back at home by nine-thirty as he has to be up early for work. I can't wait to tell Harry and Louella about our next potential client and fall asleep dreaming that I'm Kiddo from 'Kill Bill', slicing the heads off bad guys and collecting bags of cash in payment from my grateful public. I am woken at three-thirty by a clattering noise outside; I tiptoe to the window and peer into the gloomy darkness. Ed Crink is wobbling his way across the road from the house opposite - I see a downstairs light snap out and a dim flickering light, possibly a candle, appear in one of the upstairs windows. I watch him drunkenly open and then fall in through his front door. The candle-light opposite outlines the dark shadow of a person moving slowly around the room, back and forth for at least five minutes until it is suddenly extinguished. I continue to stare at the darkened window opposite and jump out of my skin when a face appears against the glass. Diving back into bed, I wonder what on earth PC Crink and Mr Creepy could have in common, other than beer.

It is an agonising two days before I see Harry and Louella again because my parents designated the weekend 'family bonding time' and wouldn't allow me or my sister to do anything that didn't involve them.

"So what's the big news," Louella asks, twizzling her straw around her cup.

"We have a new client," I state.

"Client?" Harry looks confused, "for what?"

"A pervert who needs stopping," I whisper, aware that McDonald's is probably not the most secure place to discuss our next job.

"Don't you mean VICTIM?" asks Louella.

I shrug, "Victim implies an innocent party, this guy is NOT a victim," I realise my voice has raised and I lean in to the table and add, in a hushed tone, "we don't need to kill this one, just teach him a lesson."

"So who is he?" asks Harry.

I tell them what I learned from Malcolm, which isn't really much to go on, other than the guy's name and the company he works for.

Louella munches thoughtfully on a soggy chicken nugget, "We could get into his office, fix up secret cameras to catch him in the act," she suggests.

Harry shakes his head, "We don't have spy cameras and we certainly couldn't afford to buy them."

"Actually," my mind starts whirring with crazy ideas, "we do have the money – we could spare a bit - call it re-investment."

"She's right, we could set ourselves up properly, like modern day Nancy Drews," agrees Louella.

"Great, would that make me one of the Hardy Boys?"

"Or you could be her boyfriend, Ned."

"I'm not being called Ned,"

"Can you please stop floating away in your damned books and focus on what to do next," my hands emphasise my exasperation and I accidentally send Harry's milkshake flying towards an incredibly good looking man drinking coffee two tables away. Unfortunately, he is engrossed in his phone and does not look up in-time to avoid the milky missile.

"WHAT THE FUCK!"

He is angry, but oh so handsome. I jump out of my seat, quickly shrugging off my jacket to reveal as much cleavage as possible and rush to help the poor man. Conveniently, he already has a couple of napkins and I grab them and start dabbing at his trousers. He stares down at me and I look up at him with my best apologetic-stroke-cute smile – he glowers, so I thrust out my cleavage and he is distracted. I scrub earnestly at the froth on his inner thigh.

"Stop! For god's sake stop," he slams his hands on the table.

"I'm sooo sorry…" my eyelashes flutter into overdrive and I can feel Harry and Louella glowering at me in disapproval.

He places a warm hand on my shoulder, slides it under my chin and gently pulls me upright. I widen my eyes and I see him warm to me.

"It's going to need dry-cleaning," he says.

"Of course I'll pay for it."

"Do you know how much it costs to dry-clean a suit of this quality?"

I feel he is toying with me, he is still holding me close. I shake my head.

"Seventy-five pounds," he stares pointedly at me then adds, "and that's if the stain comes out, if it doesn't you'll owe me a whole new suit."

He maintains eye contact and I feel he is daring me to ask.

"How much?"

He throws the figure out like a challenge, "About eight-hundred pounds."

Well I'm certainly not going to tell him I currently have fifteen-thousand pounds stuffed behind last year's prom dress. I raise my eyebrows in feigned horror, "But I'm a student, I don't have that kind of money."

"Don't you have a summer job?"

I had planned to start looking for one but then I killed a guy and stole his stolen money.

"Not yet," I say.

"What's your name?"

"Emily Carlton."

He smirks and I do believe that he is going all Christian Grey on me, "Well Miss Carlton, I happen to have an opening for a summer position, if you are interest?"

I nod coyly, "Are you sure?"

His phone buzzes and he glances at it, "I have to go," he pulls a card from his jacket pocket and hands it to me, "give my secretary a call - tell her I recommended you for the summer position."

He departs and I return jubilantly to my friends.

"What on earth happened there?" asks Louella.

"I got myself summer job – how's that for a turnaround?"

"Nicely done," agrees Harry, "so who are you going to be working for?"

I lay the card down on the table; it reads 'James Denton, CEO, Patcham and Co.

Mission Possible

The building is immensely tall and stark, reflecting grey clouds in its opaque glass panes. I take a tentative step towards the chrome doors and am suddenly swept through them by a tide of office workers cradling coffees and smart-phones. I arrive inside and am immediately beckoned over by a surly security guard; there is no going back now.

"Name?" his finger is poised, ready to commit my details to his device.

"Hi, my name is Emily Carlton and I'm here for…."

"Department?" he is having no idle chit-chat.

"I don't know," big mistake, his brow furrows and he reluctantly moves to the next item in the list.

Speaking very slowly, as if I must be a bit dim, "Do you know who you are going to be working for?"

Two can play at this game, "Yes."

He makes a throaty, growling sound and I quickly spit out, "James Denton, I'm here for the summer job."

He looks me up and down, smirks and turns to whisper something in the ear of a female colleague sitting behind the reception desk – I manage to catch the words '…this season's model…'. She shakes her head and makes a quiet tutting sound.

"Is there a problem?" I ask.

The woman tightens her lips and hands me a pass and the security guard tells me to follow him. We take the lift in awkward silence to the fifteenth floor, where I am led along a carpeted corridor, past five closed doors to a large office where a particularly vicious looking secretary peers over the top of her pearlescent glasses and fixes me with a prolonged stare. Her piercing eyes are hooded by thick, powder-blue lids and her scarlet lipstick is bleeding into the smoker's creases of her sun-abused skin.

I give her a wide smile but, she is unmoved by it. I reckon the security guard is probably scared of her because he has scarpered without a word.

"So, you are here for the summer?" she doesn't wait for me to confirm, "Has Mr Denton explained what your role will involve?"

She knows full well that he hasn't because I spoke to her on the telephone two days ago and told her I had no idea what the summer job involved, only that I had been offered it and had been told to speak to her. She had given nothing away on the telephone, only the briefest instructions to appear at Patcham and Co two days later and to dress in a business-like manner. She eyes me up and down, assessing my attire and gives just the hint of a satisfied sneer.

"Mr Denton is in a meeting at the moment so I suppose I will have to show you what you will be doing." She heaves her bulk out of her chair, which appears to sigh with relief as she rises.

Marjorie, which is a far too flowery name for her, takes me through the list of tasks I will be expected to perform throughout the day, as and when she or Mr Denton require. Mostly, it is delivering and fetching documents between departments, making coffee, taking telephone messages and anything else menial that neither she or Mr Denton wish to do for themselves. It suits me fine because the pay is alright and it's a great company to put on my CV, though I mustn't forget the real reason I am here – to create some sort of a 'honey-trap' for evil Mr Denton.

Harry wanted me to take all sorts of spy equipment into the office on the first day but, I told him I needed to scout the place out first, get an idea of the routine and work out the best place to locate any cameras he might acquire. As the day progresses, I realise it is going to be difficult to do anything because Marjorie watches me like a hawk.

"So, Emily Carlton. How are you enjoying your first day with us?" James Denton has crept up right behind me and as I look up from the ream of paper I am loading into the printer, his face is only an inch from mine.

I pull back in surprise, "You made me jump," I reprimand.

He gives me a boyish grin, which is incredibly handsome. Marjorie is watching from her desk in a kind of creepy, voyeuristic way. I take another step backwards and place my hands on my hips, waiting for him to move so I can finish filling the printer.

"Don't let me stop you," he says, not moving at all.

"You should move back a bit, the printer tray kicks out ink dust when I close it - I wouldn't want to be responsible for ruining another suit." He raises an eyebrow but, moves back a whole foot.

My first week passes quickly, partly because I only work until two each day. Mr Denton is rarely in the office, although when he is, he has little respect for personal space and seems to get-off on pushing boundaries in full view of Marjorie, who I learn, is actually his mother. Ew!

On Friday, I meet Mary-Kate, who only has a couple more weeks at Patcham and Co before she heads off on a month-long tour of Asia. She could be gorgeous but, chooses to drape her size-six body in hideous, beige sack-like clothing and pins – yes PINS her golden hair into a granny-knot. Marjorie likes her; she paws at her clothing and tells her to let her hair down; literally, not figuratively.

"How are you enjoying your first week here?" Mary-Kate asks.

"Hmm…" is all I can manage mid-glug until the scalding coffee I have just swigged is cool enough to swallow.

"Have you met Mr Denton yet?" she asks.

"Actually, he's the one who offered me the job."

She raises her eyebrows at me, "I thought Marjorie was dealing with summer-job applicants?"

"Oh, I didn't apply for a job – I kind of acquired it, by accident."

She looks me up and down and I feel her sack-cloth disapproving of my clinging pencil-skirt and adorable strappy heels.

"You're very pretty…and young…" she sounds condescending and I am sure she is about to give me a lecture. She looks around and pulls me close, in a confidential manner, "Mr Denton has a reputation… one that is well deserved."

She waits for me to comprehend her subtle message; I laugh and shake my head.

"What's so funny? Don't you understand? It's all very well to flirt with men like HIM but, it can go further than you may want – he can control you – ruin you!" She is wide eyed and breathing heavily.

"Are you ok?" I wonder what happened to her to cause her such anxiety. She shakes her head and takes a deep breath as we spot Marjorie squeezing through the door.

Mary-Kate busies herself in her work and I continue to rearrange piles of invoices. We don't get another opportunity to talk further but, I vow to find out what James Denton has done to upset her so much.

Louella and I meet up with Harry in the basement room of his parent's house. After a short while, his mum appears with a tray of milk and cookies. She has been doing this since we were all seven years old. It's kind of cute and kind of annoying at the same time and apparently she even did it when Harry was in a rather compromising position with his last girlfriend. Harry said she wasn't fazed and simply asked if they would prefer something with ice to drink as it seem unusually hot that day.

As soon as she heads back upstairs, Harry delves into his rucksack and pulls out three small boxes, "spy gear!" he declares with boyish delight.

He lays them out on the table that always reminds me of my grandmother's bathroom because it is topped with the same swirly, burnished-orange tiles that must have been the height of fashion back in the seventies.

"They're tiny!" exclaims Louella, "so cute."

"Easy to hide," I add.

Harry explains at length the ins and outs of each one and the ideal locations to position them. I wonder where I will actually locate them, after all, I don't know which parts of the building Denton frequents and who he might frequent them with. I am about to pack the tiny cameras in my rucksack and stand to leave but Harry pulls me back down and with great fuss, extracts a further box he has kept out of sight under the table, his 'piece de resistance'.

"It cost a fortune but, I think we could get a lot of use out of it," he says, handing the box to me.

I open the parcel to reveal a tiny, emerald brooch; circular, with a silver centre. Harry points to one of the green stones then turns the brooch over to reveal the back of the smallest camera I have ever seen.

"There's more," he says, "I can see everything the cameras capture on my computer."

He places all four devices in different parts of the room and turns on the screen of his computer. Each camera view is displayed in a section on the screen. I wave my hand and see myself from behind and in front – hmm, I stand up, yep, looking good front and back.

"Oh jeez, Em, you're so into yourself," chides Louella.

I shrug. I'm pleased with what I've got, what's the problem? Louella and I leave Harry to his screens and head back to my house for a vampire movie-fest.

Mary-Kate's Date

-- Louella's Blog: A Passion for Crime --

He just knew that her shapeless dress hid the softest, whitest, untouched breasts a man could dream of and her tightly pinned hair shouted to be released so he could grasp handfuls of it, tug at it and control her with it. Of course, what he did not know was that her virginal appearance and sweet manner was the intentional disguise for a rage so potent; she would be capable of anything.

It had taken him four months to gain her trust – slowly, painfully, he pretended not to notice her, showed her courtesies he would never normally bother with and kept himself away from all the easy lays in the office. His reputation as a womaniser was unfounded – she could see that now. He made ready to claim his prize.

-- End of blog post --

On Monday, I found out what had happened to Mary-Kate, or rather, Mary-Kate's best-friend Jean and it turns out that I am not the only one on a mission to take James Denton down.

"So what were you about to tell me the other day?" I ask Mary-Kate, the moment Marjorie leaves the office for an extended lunch break.

"It's nothing," she says, turning to head out of the office.

"It's not nothing, you were so upset the other day, something significant has happened to you and it is your duty to warn me of it, in detail, in order to protect me from anything untoward."

Mary-Kate peers at the door and I remind her that Marjorie has gone to lunch with her sister and is not expected back in the office until much later, if at all and Mr Denton flew to San Francisco this morning.

She takes a deep breath, "OK, so my best-friend Jean started an internship here at the beginning of last year – it was a really important job for her because she needed to complete six months for final credits on her degree course but, because of HIM, she only completed eight weeks and has quit the course."

"What exactly did he do?"

"It's not so much what he did, as what she DIDN'T do," said Mary-Kate.

"OK, so what didn't Jean do?" this is going to be hard going.

"Well Jean, despite her plain name, is really gorgeous and Denton started to hit on her almost as soon as she started here. She complained to Marjorie about it, not realising who she was and that's where things started to go bad. Marjorie told her that she had seen her flirting with Denton and perhaps she should be more careful with her behaviour if she didn't really mean it."

"So what did Jean say?"

"She was pretty shocked but, she thought that perhaps she had given him the wrong impression and tried her best to avoid him and started wearing less attractive clothing, which worked for a bit but then, Marjorie started to send her out to business meetings with Denton – it got really awkward, especially when Marjorie started making suggestions about her and telling other people in the office that Jean had a 'thing' for her son."

"Oh god!" I cringe, "that must have been so awkward for her."

"It got really difficult but, Jean really needed to keep the job because her parents are sick and she needs to qualify so she can get a well-paid job to support them. It got worse, though…" Mary-Kate looked like she was going to cry.

I put my hand on her arm, "Keep going, you need to get this off your chest."

Mary-Kate sniffed, "About seven weeks in, Marjorie told her she had booked Denton on an overnight business trip and Jean would be going with him. Jean was sick with worry about the trip and Marjorie kept making comments about how she must be excited to have some time alone with her handsome boss – Jean was so tempted to call in sick but, I think Marjorie had an idea she might do something like that and told her that if, for any reason, she missed the trip, that would be the end of her internship," Mary-Kate paused to take a swig of water.

I was getting impatient, "So, did Jean go or did she take a sick-day?"

"She went, although she was actually really ill, due to the stress."

"And what happened?"

"Marjorie 'forgot' to book a hotel room for Jean and of course, Denton offered to let her share his – he even promised to be the perfect gentleman and sleep on the sofa – well, she didn't have a lot of choice," Mary-Kate sounded so deflated, "anyway, Jean made it clear to him that she was not interested in him in the slightest…"

"Did he rape her?"

"Yes, well, not actual sex but, pretty much," Mary-Kate breaks into sobs and I have to console her until she is ready to finish the story, "but the worse thing was that when they got back, Marjorie had spread a vicious rumour that Denton had kindly put Jean up for the night in his room because the hotel had made a mistake with the booking and Jean had got drunk and tried to sexually assault Denton."

"Did she call the police?"

"No, HE did."

"HE called the police? But he was the one who assaulted her," I argue.

"That's what's so awful about this whole situation," sobbed Mary-Kate, "Jean is the victim, but Marjorie set her up by making the whole office believe she was obsessed with him – I think they planned the whole thing together."

"So what happened to Jean?"

"Well, Denton played the ultimate hand by showing everyone what a gentleman he was by agreeing not to press any charges. Jean took a few days off sick from stress and then just couldn't bring herself to return to Patcham and Co, especially after one of the secretaries started tweeting really horrid stuff about her."

"That's terrible, poor Jean…" I rub Mary-Kate's shoulders as she sobs again, "So why are YOU working here, for him?"

Mary-Kate peers at me for the longest time - I guess she is trying to decide whether to share her last bit of information with me, "I wanted to take revenge," she takes a really deep breath now and wipes her eyes, "I want to catch him in the act – with proof and take him down."

Well, that's a coincidence.

I suggest we take an early lunch break and head down the street to a café where I tell her all about Malcolm's mum and my current mission. Mary-Kate hugs me so hard that she almost suffocates me, which is surprising considering her tiny frame. We chat about what we could do and she tells me the different plans she had thought of but not had the opportunity or bravado to go through with but, now there are two of us…

The next day, Mary-Kate and I set up the cameras, she has a better knowledge of Denton's movements and helps me to place them in the most appropriate locations, then I phone Harry and he confirms visuals on each camera. Mary-Kate wears the brooch-camera because she spends more time with Denton, however, we still haven't decided precisely how we are going to take him down. A week later, an opportunity presents itself to us and we just have to roll with it.

To be honest, I am a teeny weeny bit jealous when Mary-Kate confides that Denton has asked her to work late that evening to help him put together a presentation for some clients – I really thought I would be the one he'd choose to hit on first, although I can see how he might go for her 'pure and virginal' act.

"Make sure the brooch is in a place where it can get a good view, if he makes a move," I suggest.

A little bit later that morning, Mary-Kate urgently drags me into the nearest stationery cupboard, "Marjorie told me Denton wants me to go to his home with him to get this presentation done, she says it could be a long evening so she has organised some food to keep us going."

I don't like the idea of Mary-Kate alone with Denton and I argue against her going but, she tells me she is willing to sacrifice herself, if necessary.

"But what will you do?"

"It depends if he tries anything on."

"Well, suppose he tries to kiss you?"

"I could slash his face with a knife."

"We need to hurt him more than that."

Mary-Kate nods in vehement agreement, "we need to make sure the camera catches him so we can get him locked up."

I shake my head, "Do you know how much money this guy has?" I've been doing my research, "He'll get a good lawyer and get out of anything you can throw at him."

"Then what can we do, if he's untouchable?"

"We hit him where it hurts – in the wallet."

"You mean blackmail?"

I nod.

"Can we give the money to Jean, to help her with her parents?"

"If we do this right, we can get enough out of him to help Jean and pay for both yours and my time on the job too."

I cancel my date with Malcolm that evening, leaving him a long, descriptive message about what I will do to him to make up for it next time we go out. He sends me an emoji of a dog panting – charming!

At six thirty, Harry is installed in his uncle's crematorium van just down the street from Denton's imposing, fake-Tudor mansion. He has an iPad hooked up to the brooch-camera and Louella is staking-out the house from the rear, where she has a fairly decent view of the living room window. They are both ready to rush in if necessary.

I decide to stay on at the offices and do a little bit of snooping, in case I can find any dirt on Denton. I notice Marjorie has dropped a small set of keys on the floor under her chair - how convenient of her. After a bit of fumbling, I find the key that opens the locked cabinet in the cupboard behind her desk. The top drawer contains six files with the oldest one being about thirteen years ago. I open the most recent file and discover the resume of a young woman, probably about the same age as Mary-Kate. I briefly scan her personal details and chuck it back in the cabinet, I do the same with another three and then pull all four back out again and frown as I try to channel my inner Nancy Drew. I pull out three files from the drawer below and lay the seven files in front of me then go to the filing cabinet in the office that has the current staff resumes.

Mary-Kate's file is near the front and I pull it open and scan through it – it has the same small red tick in the top right hand corner that the other files from the top drawer of the locked cabinet have. I pull out my own file, which does not have the tick in the corner.

I am convinced there is something untoward and after ten minutes, I think I have discovered a link between the files with ticks, including Mary-Kate's, so I Google the girl from the oldest file but, just as I receive a page of results, my phone rings urgently in my pocket, it's Louella.

"What is it, do you need me?" I snap at the phone.

"No, everything is fine," says Louella, "I was just ringing to let you know that so far nothing has happened, other than Mary-Kate having to pin a lot of pictures onto presentation boards – where are you?"

"I'm still at the office, I decided to take a look around and see if there is anything incriminating on Denton," I say.

"And have you found anything?"

"Actually, I think I may have, hang on the line a minute while I check something out on Google…"

Louella hums annoyingly into the phone as I click open a link, "Oh my God!"

"What?"

"Just wait a minute, don't put the phone down," I command as I grab the other two files from the top drawer and type the names into Google. My heart is pounding and I squeak something garbled to Louella.

"What? What are you saying, talk slowly," she complains.

I put my hand on my chest to try and slow my hammering heart, "I found the keys to Marjorie's filing cabinet and in one of the drawers are files of female employees – young, like interns. Each one has a red tick-mark at the top of the page and according to their personal details, they are all orphans or estranged from their families."

"So, what does that mean?"

"Well, the three I just Googled are no longer with us."

I hear Louella inhale sharply on the other end of the line, "Dead?"

"Two disappeared without trace and one was found dead at her apartment – the coroner states heart attack, possibly induced by stress as the cause of death."

"Is Mary-Kate an orphan?" asks Louella.

I grab Mary-Kate's file and read the personal details to her, "No siblings, one parent deceased, the other parent is unknown. No spouse, zero dependants."

"Em, you need to call the police, we need to get her out of there!" shrieks Louella.

"But what would we say to the cops, Denton hasn't done anything to her and we can hardly accuse him of a bunch of murders without any evidence and besides, Mary-Kate wants revenge at ANY cost."

"We can't let him kill her!"

"No, we'll stop it before it comes to that but, we need get some evidence, something to hang him with first – keep watching her, I'll join you as soon as I've put these files away."

I shakily shove the filing back where I found it, lock the cabinet and throw the keys carelessly under Marjorie's chair before leaving the office as casually as I can. Thankfully, I was able to borrow Mum's car for our mission this evening.

When I finally creep into Denton's backyard, Louella is a quivering wreck and hopping from foot to foot because she needs to pee.

"For god's sake, just go behind the bushes there, no-one can see you," she tries to balk at my inelegant but obvious solution to her discomfort then urgently leaps behind a large vine.

"Oh, thank goodness for that, I couldn't hold it for much longer," she admits gratefully on her return, "What are we going to do now?"

"Watch and wait," I say as calmly as I can.

About an hour later, a car turns up and Marjorie steps out. She is holding what looks like a casserole dish and a large carrier bag from the local hardware store. Shortly after, I feel my phone vibrate in my pocket and

I read Harry's message telling me that Mary-Kate is sitting down to eat with Denton and Marjorie. Talking of food, I'm getting really hungry and cold.

"I don't think anything untoward is going to happen tonight," I say to Louella.

"How can you be sure?" she asks.

"Look, Harry is watching through the camera, I think we can sneak off for a bite to eat – he'll let us know if we're needed."

"I am pretty hungry and bloody freezing," admits Louella.

We sneak off in my car and are soon warming ourselves up with hot chocolate and cherry-pie. An hour later, my phone vibrates again. 'I've lost visuals and I haven't seen Mary-Kate leave the house yet' is the slightly worrying message from Harry.

I dial his number, "What do you mean, lost?"

"One minute I could see her clearing her plate to the kitchen, then the screen went black, like someone had covered up the camera – it's still connected, or I would see screen-static, it's just covered up with something."

"Do you think Mary-Kate could have covered it up by accident?" I ask.

"Highly unlikely, given the circumstances," answers Harry.

"Can you still hear them?" I ask.

"Yes, I can hear voices but, they are pretty muffled so I haven't been able to make out much of what they've been saying," admits Harry.

"We're on our way back – five minutes…"

"Hurry," urges Harry, "I'm worried – I've just heard a high-pitched sound."

"What? Like a scream?" Louella grabs hold of the steering-wheel as I gesticulate my panic and press my foot harder on the accelerator.

Abandoning all subtlety, I park as close to Denton's house as possible, Louella and I leap into the back garden. Standing against the back fence, we ponder our next move.

Suddenly Louella shrieks, "We need to get in and I know how."

I frantically shush her and she points to the greenery where she relieved herself earlier, "I saw a trapdoor there, perhaps it leads to a cellar that we can use to access the house."

Personally, I think we should try ground-floor doors first but Louella's suggestion could work – so long as we don't have to trawl through her pee-puddle.

The door opens easily and we creep down a surprisingly steep and long flight of metal stairs, carefully, so as not to slip, until we reach the concrete bottom. It is dark, except for a horizontal slit of light parallel to the floor. Satisfied we are the only ones in the room, I swipe my flashlight app, and gasp.

We hear footsteps approach the door and tuck ourselves nervously under the stairwell. The door opens and a dim, red lightbulb is switched on. In the crimson glow, we survey what we momentarily glimpsed with my phone-light – restraint chairs, wall mounted handcuffs, leather straps, whips and silver-service trays laden with the sort of things Louella likes to read about. She grasps my hand and squeezes painfully as two figures enter the room. We can't see the detail but, it looks like Denton and his mother.

Marjorie fusses around at the side of the room while Denton picks up one of the strips of leather and leaves the room. Louella looks at me quizzically and I signal to her that we should hold tight. Denton returns to the room with Mary-Kate in tow, literally! She staggers in and he pushes her roughly onto a chair in the middle of the room.

We see now why the camera brooch is seeing nothing – her clothes have been replaced by a leather apron and her feet are bare. Denton ties her hands using the straps on the chair. Mary-Kate doesn't put up any kind of a fight, in fact she is totally compliant and her head is lolling around as if she has been drugged. Denton strokes her face tenderly, leaning in and thrusting eagerly against the leather apron. His mother looks up and from whatever she has been busy doing and scolds him.

She steps out of the darkness and walks towards Denton, waving a whip menacingly at him, "Sorry mummy," he whimpers.

My heart is pounding like never before and I am petrified we will be discovered but, I shuffle around so I can use my phone to film whatever is about to occur. For the next five minutes, I record Majorie strip off to reveal the sort of outfit that a woman of her age and bulk should never wear, Denton proves that he will do absolutely anything his vile mother desires and I nearly vomit all over Louella. Fortunately, Mary-Kate is untouched and only has to bear catatonic witness to the sordid events played out before her. Just as my phone is about to die, Denton whispers something in Mary-Kate's ear and both he and his mother exit the room.

Louella and I leap into action and rush to undo Mary-Kate, who feebly proclaims she is needed for the next game. Miraculously, we manage to drag her fairly quietly up the metal staircase and out of the trapdoor.

Harry is waiting for us in the van, looking distressed, "I thought you had all been horribly murdered," he exclaimed.

"So what did you do about it?" I rasp.

"I was going to call the police, in about ten more minutes," he admitted.

"Ten more minutes and we all would have been Denton's gimps."

He looks at me, not comprehending, "Look at Mary-Kate!" I shriek, as Louella struggles to push her naked ass into the van.

"What the fuck is she wearing?" he never uses that kind of language.

"Precisely," I smirk, "and the best thing is, we have it all on film, now drive. Please."

The Devil's Rose Garden

-- Louella's Blog: A Passion for Crime --

She couldn't see anything through the silk binding covering her eyes and she nearly tripped as he man-handled her down the clanking metal staircase. The room felt cold and the stone floor he lowered her onto was gritty and uncomfortable.

"You trust me, don't you?" he asked.

"I'm trying really hard to," she admitted, wondering if she should have let him read so much of her EL James.

He pulled her forward, tipped her chin and drizzled champagne over her lips until she opened her mouth willingly. He pressed himself into her, allowing her to grip his buttocks tightly, then pulled away and fed her more champagne. She was beginning to feel tipsy. She felt him pull her upright and lean her against a cold wall, he tied her arms with leather straps and spread her legs, rubbing something cold and metallic between them until she started to tremble with pleasure.

He moved away from her and she begged him to come back. She could hear him grunting with pleasure on the other side of the room. It turned her on even more. Desperate to watch him pleasure himself, she pulled hard on the restraints and managed to free an arm. She could hear his moans become more frantic and she felt herself on the brink of orgasm. She pulled her eye mask down. Her jaw dropped and every emotion she had felt a moment ago, every sensation - her near orgasm, turned to chilling, bitter, disgust.

"Your MOTHER!"

-- End of blog post --

We go to Louella's house, her parents are at counselling, which is usually followed by a visit to a Premier Inn, to act out whatever bizarre task their sexual counsellor has given them.

I lay Mary-Kate on the chintzy sofa while Louella finds some clothes to put on her and Harry just sits and watches, jaw dropped, at the footage we took.

"I'm going to need counselling myself after watching this," complains Harry, "and you say that's his MOTHER?"

I nod.

"He REALLY loves her, doesn't he?"

I nod again.

"So what do we do? Do we kill him?" asks Louella, as she tries to manoeuvre a purple thong over Mary-Kate's inert legs.

"We should blackmail him," I suggest.

"What if he doesn't go for it?" asks Harry, "the video only shows him and Marjorie, it doesn't show Mary-

Kate tied up. Doing…uh, THAT with your mother, disgusting as it is, isn't actually illegal."

"Don't you think that will be enough?"

"It would have been better if you had a kidnap victim in the video too."

Shit! I should've thought of that, "Perhaps we can Photoshop her in?" I suggest.

Harry gives me that look.

"We have to do something," pleads Louella, "Don't forget there are other girls that he probably killed."

"Perhaps we could find out where they are and dig one up, he'd definitely be more susceptible to blackmail then," I suggest.

"And how are you going to find the bodies?" asks Harry

"I expect he buried them in the garden, under the roses," says Louella, "he seems like the kind of person who would like to keep his conquests close and arrogant enough to believe no-one would ever find them."

"Seriously, that's such a cliché?"

"Well, it wouldn't hurt to take a look," says Harry.

"And you think it's going to be that easy? A man who has probably gotten away with several murders over the last two decades is going to be harder to crack than that!" I protest.

"Fine," says Louella, "you stay here then and me and Harry will go and take a look in his garden."

"He won't be there," says Harry, matter-of-factly, "he'll either be out looking for Mary-Kate, or hiding somewhere waiting to see if she's been to the police."

"What if he goes into hiding for good? Then we'll never be able to blackmail him," I complain.

"Put me back."

We turn simultaneously to see Mary-Kate attempting to sit up on the sofa, "put me back at the house, I want us to get the bastard."

The drugs haven't worn off yet and she is still failing to control her head but, her eyes are focussed and she appears to be mentally lucid.

"But…"

"No buts, we don't have time…" Mary-Kate looks like she might vomit, "help me get this thong back off."

Reluctantly, we shove Mary-Kate back into the van, then out of the van and leave her to wander drunkenly at the back of Denton's garden, as though she had accidentally ended up there through her own efforts. Of course, Harry is right, Denton's car is nowhere to be seen.

The three of us hide in Denton's garden. We can hear Mary-Kate scuffing around the fence behind us and I really hope no other pervert spots her in her leather apron.

We hear a car pull up at the fence, whispered voices then the garden gate opens and I thank god it is dark as we watch Denton lead Mary-Kate along the winding garden path to the back door of the house. She is doing a great job of acting drugged and compliant. As soon as she and Denton enter the house, Louella and Harry decide that I will be the one to check the garden and they enter via the trapdoor ready to spring Mary-Kate free again, once they have got sufficient camera footage.

I take the opportunity to wander through the large and ornately planted garden. Evidently Denton is a bit of a plant nerd, he has actual metal plaques on each flowerbed, naming the plants within it. I read the first one and take a sharp intake of breath – I mean, REALLY! Is he THAT arrogant?

According to the label, the rose in this bed is called Absent Friends.

I move on to the next bed and see that the roses are called Sophia and Chloe, which match with two of the interns in the filing cabinet. A chill runs through me and I really want to get the hell out of here but, my inquisitive nature pushes me on. There are three beds of strange and exotic looking grasses but, none of them with suspicious names, however, the last bed I come to is once again filled with roses and, according to the plaque, they are Elizabeth and Meg. Jeez, I wonder if he only goes for girls with rose-type names?

I make a note of the girl's names on my phone and ponder digging a little but, it's dark, Denton is at home and I only have my bare hands so I go back to the trap-door entrance and wait.

"Oh my god! Oh my god! Oh my god!" shrieks Louella's voice from the rising trapdoor. She stumbles into my arms whimpering.

"What's the matter?" I demand sharply.

"She, Ma-Marjorie…the devil, she's the devil!"

Louella has lost it, I drop her sagging body against the fence, take a deep breath and think; what would Buffy the Vampire Slayer do? I grab a pair of rusty garden shears and a terracotta plant pot that have been conveniently left there and head down the steep staircase, no longer concerned about making a noise.

I am prepared to face whatever but, the scene in front of me is confusing. The air is thickly scented and Harry appears to be in some kind of a trance and is slowly gesticulating his hips around Marjorie's enormous rear. Mary-Kate has passed out again and has been laid on the floor over a chalk-drawn pentagram and Denton is sprinkling what looks like salt over her. Weirder still, no one notices me.

As Marjorie shifts her significant bulk, I see that she is wearing some kind of devil mask and is clasping a glinting knife to her chest. The candles in the room flicker and their shadows dance menacingly. Shit! What the hell am I supposed to do?

Film! Get it on record, preserve the evidence.

I video fervently, some of which I know Harry will want me to delete as I record him unzipping his trousers and, ew, no! I tune my focus on Denton and his salt sprinkling, to which he has now added chanting. The room appears to darken further as his chanting and Marjorie's ecstatic moaning reach a feverish pitch. My skin prickles and I really want to get the hell out of here.

Mary-Kate begins to shudder and writhe like she is having an orgasm and Denton kneels down between her legs. He pulls a long knife from under his shirt and I almost faint…must hold on, they are relying on me.

He slides the knife along the inside of her thigh then raises it high above her chest. Harry grunts loudly and I leap from the stairs, pushing Denton away from Mary-Kate. Marjorie is oblivious as Harry thrusts against her, then suddenly, she makes this weird guttural sound and begins to ramble in some foreign language – possibly Latin. Denton still has the knife, so I fling the plant pot as hard as I can at his head. He drops like a sack of potatoes. Marjorie carries on with her strange rambling then she too passes out on the floor.

Harry looks up at me blankly, then I watch as the realisation of what has been going on hits him, "Seriously, no? I wasn't…I couldn't have been, it was a dream…nightmare, wasn't it?" he pleads.

I shake my head and waggle the phone at him.

"You didn't?"

I nod.

"We need to get out of here," he says, looking around in panic, "where's Lou?"

I point up the stairs and he breathes a sigh of relief, then a look of panic, "Did she see…?"

"I don't think so."

Harry gently lifts Mary-Kate, leaving a Mary-Kate shaped salt outline on the floor, like a murder scene. I carefully pull Denton's arm from under him and feel for a pulse. Unfortunately, he still has one so I follow Harry up the stairs. At least we don't have another body to burn.

We head back to Louella's and manage to get there before her parents do, giving us time to dress Mary-Kate and shake her back into consciousness. Harry and I head to his house where we can watch the videos properly and decide what to do.

An hour later, just before midnight we have made a plan; Harry has deleted a couple of scenes, made four copies of the remaining footage and put two on a CD, one in a Dropbox account and emailed another to one of his many Gmail accounts.

We type a short letter enclosing one of the CDs, Harry immediately drives off and delivers the envelope to Denton's post-box.

Five days later, we collect a leather holdall containing five-hundred thousand pounds from a coach station locker.

We have enough money to save little Aiden and a nice bonus for each for us, Mary-Kate and her friend Joan.

Louella and I take the bag of cash into the ladies loo and stuff all but Aiden's two-hundred thousand pounds into our backpacks – it takes forever to count and we get a rather suspicious look from the cleaning attendant when we emerge together from the same stall.

"Do you think she knows?" asks Louella.

"I think it's more likely, she thinks we were 'getting it on'," I tell her, "judging by the way she winked at me."

"God, how embarrassing!" exclaims Louella.

"Seriously, with all the stuff you write and what your parents get up to – THAT embarrasses you?"

"No!" she shakes her head wildly, "it's the thought that I might do that sort of thing in a DISGUSTING toilet," she explains.

"Oh," what more can I say?

We put Denton's case, containing the money for Aiden into a new locker then go home and write a note that says, 'All you need to make Aiden better', along with the locker location and combination. We post it to the address on the card Aiden's sisters gave us with the cookies.

Life is good. Then two police cars pull up outside my house.

Cashing In

-- Louella's Blog: A Passion for Crime --

The uniform gave him so much authority and I was compelled to bend entirely to his will. He cuffed me, I knew I had done bad things, but he cuffed me gently, fixing the clasps and then caressing my fingers before turning me gently towards the wall for the pat-down. We both knew I wasn't concealing anything, other than lust, but he made a point of checking each and every crevice with a firm hand.

As he leaned up to reach my arms, his gun pressed into the small of my back and I whimpered…

-- End of blog post --

I watch from the window as a particularly hot police officer climbs out of the car, casually adjusts his belt and pushes back his hair. He reminds me of that cheesy cop show mum once showed me – CHIPS, the tanned one with a really weird name but, oh boy was he HOT. Jeez, I can't believe I'm crushing on a bloke that is most likely going to cuff me then roughly shove me into the back of his car…ooh stop - he's going to take me to jail. They know what we did!

I grab my phone to text Louella and Harry but realise I would be incriminating myself further. I peek out of the window again, he's about to knock on the door, I need to get a grip.

Mum gets to the door first and I wait at the top of the stairs, listening so hard I feel like my ears are going to pop off my head.

"Hello, can I help you?"

"Good afternoon madam, we're trying to get information about a local family - they've been conning a lot of people out of money, we are trying to ascertain just how many people may have been affected by this crime."

I creep a little further down the stairs, increasingly confident that they are not after me.

"…apparently, they've been sending two of their foster children to people's houses selling cookies and asking them to donate money to send their fictitious son for cancer treatment, it looks like they were pretty convincing – they've managed to accumulate at least twenty-thousand pounds."

So, the cops don't know about the two-hundred thousand pounds we gave them – perhaps they haven't picked it up yet. I am furious! How could they con us like this – we would have killed for poor little Aiden and now we find out he's not even real.

I make my excuses to mum and dart out of the house. As I reach the end of our driveway, I notice Mr Creepy from opposite is standing in his window, staring. I stare back. He does that really creepy 'I'm watching you' thing with his fingers. Shit! Does he know?

I try to walk nonchalantly but somehow feel I am giving off 'guilty' vibes. Harry meets me halfway to Louella's house on his bike and I tell him what happened. His face pales and he grips my hand tightly – I hope no one sees us, they might think Harry is my boyfriend and much as I love him as a friend, he is nowhere near the sort of guy I would date.

Louella ushers us into her house, frantically shushing us as we sneak into the den. I frown but, she points up and makes an obscene gesture. The light fitting on the ceiling above us sways as floorboards groan rhythmically. I guess her parents have had more counselling.

Harry and I explain the situation to her and she looks really worried.

"What about the note we sent them, what if the cops find it – they'll know about the money and wonder where it came from and when they realise it's from a bunch of teens, they'll want to know how we got it."

"Just how long are your parents going to keep that up for?" I enquire.

"Dad's got Viagra, so it could be a while."

"Let's get out of here," I suggest, "they're beginning to affect me."

Harry nods in understanding, "do they do this a lot?"

Louella nods, "you can go and watch through the keyhole in their door if you like."

Harry shares my revulsion, "Seriously? That's kinda sick, watching your own parents at it."

Louella shrugs, "It's not only them, sometimes mum does it with the sex counsellor too, he's really cute and he's got the most enormous…"

"Louella!"

"God, you're such a prude Em."

We take a walk down the tree-lined road and head to a local park where we sit under a tree, away from the squealing toddlers and yapping dogs.

"We need to get back the note we sent them," says Harry.

"And retrieve the money before they collect it," I add.

"The letter may not have reached them yet – you know how slow the post is," suggests Louella, "or perhaps they haven't collected it yet because they know they are under investigation?"

"We need to go by their house and see if they are still there, or if they've been arrested yet," says Harry.

"How will we know? And what if the police are watching the house?" I counter.

"I don't know but, we need to try," says Harry.

We decide that Louella will go and retrieve the cash from the coach station; she will wear one of her mum's wigs and sunglasses and only go in when new coach full of people are unloading, so she is less likely to be spotted.

"Why does your mum have wigs?" asks Harry.

"She's into role-play, especially when she goes on date-nights with Dad," Louella explains, as if it is a perfectly natural thing to do.

Harry is going to cycle past the house after dark, that way he'll be able to see if there are any lights on and be less likely to be spotted. His phone rings, making us all jump guiltily.

"Shit, I'm needed at work, Uncle Albert has stiffs to collect and he needs me to help lift them into the van – his sciatica's playing up."

He heads off on his creaky bike while Louella and I head back to her house to collect a wig and glasses, then to my house to borrow mum's car.

We drive past the coach station, it's completely dead, so we continue by and stop to get a burger. On the second drive past it is still empty, but I spot a couple of coaches about to turn in. Louella jumps out and joins the milling throng as they escape from their cramped seats. She has the lock code written on her wrist, in case her nerves cause her to forget it in the heat of the moment.

After about ten minutes I scan the crowd for her and my heart nearly stops when I notice a police car pull up at the other end of the building. They enter the station and my knees begin to shake – 'COME ON Louella, hurry!' My mind pleads.

Five minutes later, she has the audacity, or stupidity, to saunter out carrying our holdall like there is not urgency whatsoever.

"What the hell are you playing at?" I shriek at her, "you were supposed to grab the bag and run."

"If it was there," says Louella.

"Well, it obviously was, didn't you see the cops?"

"Yes," says Louella.

She has always been infuriating, but this is about her worst moment.

"Did they see you?"

She shakes her head, "I had a really good view of them well before they came into the building – I had a moment of inspiration that will cover us even if they have seen the letter."

"I think we can assume they have." I say wryly, "So what was this genius idea?"

"I put a note in the locker."

"You did WHAT?"

"I wrote a note on a piece of paper that said, 'Just kidding!'"

"How the hell is that supposed to help us?"

"It's a sick joke but, the cops will then assume there never was any money in the first place and they're not going to investigate a non-crime, even if it is a sick joke."

"You think?" it sounds like a good idea but I need convincing.

"Well, I waited and watched them open the locker," I shake my head in disapproval, "they read the note, shook their heads in disgust and threw it in the bin – if they thought there was any more to it than that, they would have kept the note and gone to look at the CCTV footage."

She's right, thank goodness, so now we have the cash again and we're off the hook. Louella puts the holdall on the back seat of the car and we clamber in. The stress has left me feeling faint and I rest my head on the steering-wheel, Louella is busy texting Harry with the news when we both jump in surprise as the rear door of the car clicks open and an arm reaches in and grabs the bag.

"Hey!" yells Louella, leaping from her seat, grabbing the bag and pushing the man to the ground.

She leaps back into the car, "DRIVE!"

"Jeez Louella, I never knew you were Kickass, that was awesome!"

"I feel sick, I think the adrenaline is getting to me," she groans.

I drive as fast as I can back to my house and sneak the bag and a shaking Louella up to my bedroom. I tiptoe back downstairs again and double-check everyone else is out before grabbing two glasses from the kitchen and pouring myself and Louella a hefty shot of whiskey from my mum's spare bottle under the sink.

Louella nurses her drink while I glug my entire shot down in one – god, that feels good.

I hear a car pull up on the neighbours drive and a door slam. I clamber off the bed and see Ed Crink staring at my car. He scratches his head and peers through the rear window then looks up towards my bedroom. Fortunately, I am standing far enough back that I don't think he can see me. I watch him walk back over to his own car, sit down in the driver's seat and take out his mobile.

About ten minutes later, I hear another car pull up outside his house. Crink, who hasn't moved from his vehicle, jumps out and goes to talk to the driver. There is a raised voice, I'm not sure if it is Crink or the unseen car driver, then the car screeches off and Crink slinks back up his front path and lets himself into his house.

There is something going on, something that is making me feel really uneasy. Louella is fast asleep, having finally downed her drink and I don't want to wake her after her earlier shock, besides, I have a date with Malcolm in a couple of hours, so I run a hot bath.

As I lay back on the cushion of foam, I drift into a whiskey infused dream about Malcolm stripping off to reveal his superbly toned torso, sliding down his trunks to reveal…

"Oh my god!" I sit up abruptly, raising a tidal wave of bubbles that spill onto the floor, "what the hell are you doing?"

"Oh come on, we always used to share baths when we were kids," says Louella, weaving her legs between mine, "besides, it looked like you were having a lovely fantasy there," she smirks, "want to tell me all about it?"

"Louella, this is kinky – even for you."

"Don't you remember when we used to scrub each other's backs?" she asks.

"Yes and we also had Barbie-dolls and plastic fish!" I remind her.

She gives me one of her pleading, puppy-dog looks and obligingly, just for old times-sake and to shut her up I swivel myself around and lean forward. Louella soaps her hands and massages my back and shoulders, I feel the knots begin to unwind and I moan in appreciation, which Louella evidently takes the wrong way as she begins to slide her hot soapy hands around my breasts. I'll admit it feels incredibly good, but that is probably because of the whiskey - and the guilt.

"Louella, I thought you liked boys?" I am genuinely confused.

"Oh I do, it's just I feel so wound up, so tense from everything that's happened today."

"Why don't you just ask Harry to, uh, help you out – you know he's absolutely desperate to?"

"That's the problem, he's desperate and so am I and I wouldn't be able to trust myself to not – you know?" I can feel her whole body resting against mine and the warmth is lovely.

"Are you really going to save yourself for marriage?"

"Yep, I intend to be a virgin on my wedding night, it'll be so romantic."

"I'm pretty sure that also involves not getting down and dirty with your best friend – or anything else for that matter."

"Get real," she laughs, "I'll be a technical virgin."

I sigh heavily as Louella continues to rub her soapy hands over me and swear to add this to the list of things I have done this summer that must never be mentioned again. Ever.

Love is Dead

-- Louella's Blog: A Passion for Crime --

'He stared down at her immaculate torso, admired the gleaming white skin against the navy, silk spread. Her lips were painted a glossed cherry-red; plump mouth parted a little to reveal the tips of her perfect teeth. You could barely notice the crack where he had carefully mended the one that broke when she fell off the table. In fact, he was so pleased with his work that instead of gluing her lips together, he had arranged them just so and glued them to her teeth. He was thrilled with the effect. His favourite cadaver to date...'

-- End of blog post --

My date with Malcolm is great, we have a lovely time and I forget all about my stresses. He is the ultimate gentleman throughout our dinner and even bowling afterwards but, on our way back to my car, he practically jumps on me and kisses me passionately, pinning me against the side of the car and pressing himself against me.

"Malcolm, you're usually such a gentleman!" I admonish.

"I'm sorry Em, I couldn't help, you looked so damn hot all night."

He looks truly apologetic and pulls back from me, I giggle and lean in for another deep kiss. This time, he ventures his hands up my skirt – which is so short that there really isn't much distance to the goal. I let him linger a moment, then whisper in his ear. He groans in anticipation.

"I thought you were joking when you sent that text to me," he says, "that's why I sent the tacky, panting dog emoticon."

"I'm no tease," I whisper.

"Oh, but you are, you've been teasing me for so long…"

He is seriously beginning to lose control.

"Are you, have you, er, I mean…" he is trying to be delicate, bless him and I hate to disappoint him.

"Yes," I whisper, "I'm a virgin," the poor boy is nearly crumpling at the knees, I prop him up, "so, where can we go?"

Malcolm looks forlornly at my car, "it's a bit small, I wish mine wasn't off the road,"

"It also belongs to my mother," I really should date older guys, with apartments, or at least decent cars.

"Oi, get a room!"

What the hell is Harry doing here? He drives his van into the bowling alley car park and leans out of the window, "gonna meet some guys for a game, where are you young lovers heading?"

I shrug my shoulders at him, "my parents are home."

"So are mine," adds Malcolm.

"Do you uh, want a pad to uh, crash for a bit?" he asks.

"What, your place?"

"No, my olds are in for the night too but, I've got the keys to the office and there's no one there till the morning."

Malcolm is already getting into the car but I grab him by the shoulder, "you do realise where Harry's office is, don't you?"

"Does it matter?"

"He works at the crematorium."

"Oh."

"Oh come on, the office is at the front of the building, you won't have to go anywhere near any stiffs," says Harry.

I raise my eyebrows and Malcolm stifles a snigger.

"Seriously, do you want the keys? You could drop them back here to me in about an hour."

"You don't have CCTV at your office do you?"

Harry laughs, "No, no CCTV, no security and no alarms."

I look at Malcolm, who nods an eager yes and Harry flings him the keys, "It's two blocks up, on the right – you can't miss it."

Malcolm is back in the car, eager for me to get going. We drive the short road to Harry's Uncle's crematorium. I've never been in a crematorium at night – or even in the day for that matter. This day has gone from deeply scary to deeply kinky on a grand scale.

Despite there being no-one but the dead in here, Malcolm puts his finger to his lips as he unlocks he door and we creep along the corridor to a plush office with a large settee and a massive box of tissues. How convenient.

Malcolm leads me to the desk and pushes me against it. So not the comfy sofa then.

"Do you think there are any ghosts here?" I ask, probably inappropriately, considering Malcolm is about to unzip his jeans.

"What?"

"Nothing," I really shouldn't distract him, "it's just that a light seemed to flicker on outside the room." I point to the door, where a faint strip of light is now glowing through.

"Harry said there wasn't anyone here tonight; it's probably just a security light."

I'm sure he's right. He pushes against me and I squeeze my legs around him.

"I'll take it slowly," whispers Malcolm, already pressing for entry. I'm beginning to wonder if this is actually HIS first time.

"You do have protection, don't you?" I ask.

"Shit! No, I uh, do you?"

Oh god, this is his first time and it's going to be over in seconds.

I push Malcolm away, then realise my bag is still in the car.

"I'll go get it," offers Malcolm.

There is no way I'm being left on my own in the crematorium, "I'll come with you."

The light that flickered on is still burning brightly further down the hall and it looks like another light has come on in one of the rooms further down too. I nudge Malcolm, he shrugs his shoulders and I indicate we should take a look. Wordlessly, we tiptoe towards the illuminated door and peer through the small, rectangular window in it.

The image is distorted by the glass, but what I see is enough, more than enough. I feel sick; Malcolm is shaking his head violently, as if to dislodge the image from his brain. I am about to grab his hand to make a speedy exit when I have an idea – I'm beginning to think like a private detective and you never know when one might need to leverage someone to do you a favour.

I grab my phone from my pocket; thank god I never, ever leave that in my bag! I put the phone up to the window and video for at least a minute before Malcolm pulls me away. We exit the building, climb into my car and drive shakily away.

"Who was that?" asks Malcolm.

"I presume it must be good old Uncle Albert," I say, "I think only he and Harry work there."

"He is one sick bastard!"

"There seem to be a lot of them," I say.

"Do you know other people like him?" asks Malcolm.

Oops, I must be more careful with my words, "Oh, just what I read in the paper – there are perverts everywhere."

"Not like that," he exclaims.

"Well, I guess not many guys have access to a crematorium."

"Why did you video him?"

Hmm, good question – how to answer that one… "I don't really know, I er, I guess I thought I might need to show Harry what his uncle gets up to – I'm not sure if he'd believe me if I told him."

"You're going to show that to him?"

"Maybe,"

"I think we had better go home," says Malcolm, who has most definitely gone off the boil.

I drop him off at his house and then head back down to the bowling alley, intending to go in and show Harry the video but instead, sit in the car park for ten minutes mulling it over. I decide to leave it for the moment and switch the engine on to head back home.

Halfway back home, I realise I still have the keys to the crematorium, so I turn back around and once again head to the bowling alley. I spot Harry coming out with two other guys. I beep the horn and he spots me and heads over.

"So, how was your postie, did he deliver?" Harry thinks he is hilarious.

"Actually, things didn't really go according to plan," I start.

Harry climbs into the passenger seat and looks at me expectantly. He's going to get some juicy details, but not the ones he's expecting.

Fake Agents

I leave Harry to mull over what I've just shown him, drive home and fall into bed in an exhausted heap. I wake the following morning bright and chirpy from a sound night of sleep to find a note shoved under my bedroom door. It is in a sealed envelope which bears no markings. I wonder if it's from my idiot sister; she's done it before, once when she borrowed one of my favourite dolls and then dropped its head down a drain hole, she wrote me a really sweet note apologising and offering to give me her pocket money for the next five weeks to make up for it.

The letter isn't from Frances.

'I want my money back'

That's all it says, no name, no address, no indication of who 'I' is, which is a problem because it could be associates of the deceased perv from under my bed, Mr Denton and his beloved mother or possibly even fake-Aiden's parents. As I ponder the sender of the letter, it suddenly hits me; whoever 'I' is, knows where I live and, urgh... I shudder, crept into the house last night.

I text Harry and Louella to meet me, urgently.

Louella looks like she's about to faint when I tell her about the note. Harry suggests I call the police then, realizes how dumb that would be.

"Did they say how they want us to return the money?" asks Harry.

I shake my head.

"Or who, because it makes a difference – we don't want to be returning two-hundred thousand when they might only be expecting fifteen, and how are we supposed to return it?" asks Louella.

"I guess they'll tell us, one way or another," I answer.

"I don't think it's Denton – we've got him pretty tightly sewn up," says Harry.

"What about fake-Aiden's parents, aren't they being watched by the police?" says Louella.

"And they never actually HAD the money, so they probably wouldn't say they want their money BACK, just 'we want our money'," adds Harry.

"So by that reckoning, it has to be The Associates," says Louella dramatically.

"The Associates? It makes them sound like some sort of film baddie," I feel surreal, "perhaps they'll all seem a bit less intimidating if we refer to them with film-style titles."

"Well, there's the Fake-Aidens, The Associates and…" says Harry.

"And the Beloved Dentons," laughs Louella.

"Marvellous," I shake my head in wonder at our predicament, then almost fall off the bed as my mother yells up the stairs that there are two men at the door to see me. Shit! I contemplate jumping out of the window but, whoever they are, they probably have someone waiting for me to do just that.

"It's probably nothing," says Louella, not looking like it could be nothing.

Harry shakes his head, "You'll have to go down there, they wouldn't just come to the front door if they were going to do anything bad," he reasoned, "and besides, you live next door to a cop."

I suddenly recall how Ed Crink was looking weirdly at my car after we brought the loot home, and that other guy who pulled up and spoke to him. I really, really don't want to go down the stairs but, my mother is calling again, rather insistently.

"Coming," I call as fake-cheerfully as possible, "I was just in the bathroom."

The men at the bottom of the stairs are dressed in matching suits, neat fitting but not expensive – I can tell because the buttons have a cheap shine to them and the cuff of the jacket on the taller of the two men is too short and vice versa on the shorter guy. Neither is particularly good looking and they are not smiling.

"Hi," I display my most winning and innocent smile.

My mother looks at me and touches me on the arm, "These gentlemen are CID officers, they want to talk to you about your job at Patcham and Co."

"I quit."

"We are aware of that but, you may be able to help us with an investigation we are conducting into a missing woman."

"Oh, who?" I bet it's one of the girls on the list in Denton's drawer, oh god, I hope they can't read my expression – must act shocked when they tell me.

"A Miss Calabrese, Mary-Kate, you may have met her, we believe you were there at the same time as her."

"I, er, yes, I was."

"Her handbag was found abandoned near her home a few days ago and no one seems to be able to locate her."

"Oh my goodness, I thought she was going to Asia for a month."

"Her passport was found in her apartment."

"Oh, you can't get to Asia without a passport can you?"

They both shake their heads, somewhat condescendingly, I feel.

"What can my daughter do to help you Mr…?" asks my mother, addressing the taller agent and placing a protective hand on my arm.

He doesn't give a name, "We just need to find out as much about Miss Calabrese's likely movements and the people she may have associated with, if you can tell us anything we don't already know."

"What do you think might have happened to her?" asks my mother.

"We are concerned that she may have been kidnapped."

"Why would you come to that conclusion?" she probes, "were there signs of a struggle, did someone see something that might indicate that there had been foul play?"

The officers steel my mother with an icy stare worthy of that strange melty robot in the Terminator films, "Madame, it came to our attention that Miss Calabrese was in possession of an unusually large amount of money and we are concerned that her disappearance may have something to do with that."

My mother is not letting this up, "do you think someone tried to rob her?"

"The money is in her bank account, we are concerned about where she may have acquired that money and that perhaps it has led to her being in a perilous situation."

"You are merely speculating at this point," presses my mother, "you have no evidence?"

"No."

"Do you believe there is any reason for my daughter to be concerned for her own safety, should your concerns prove valid?"

"At this point, we do not think so," he pauses, then looks straight at me, "unless of course, she also has a large sum of money and disappears unexpectedly."

And the penny drops; these are not CID officers, these guys are representatives of the 'I' in the letter which is currently burning a hole in my back pocket. They have taken Mary-Kate and are threatening to kidnap me too, if I don't return their money.

"Well she certainly doesn't have any money hidden away – if she did, she wouldn't keep trying to borrow money from me," laughs my mother – god how inappropriate given the situation, "Emily, is there any information that you can give these gentlemen about Miss Calabrese?"

"No, I only worked with her a couple of times; I didn't really get to know her."

The agents stand up. The taller one pulls a piece of paper out of a notepad, writes down a telephone number and hands it to me, "Call us if you think of anything."

The effort required for me not to shake violently when I take the note from him leaves me unable to speak, so I nod as smoothly as I can while my mother ushers them out of the door.

"Well, they weren't very friendly, were they?" she exclaims loudly, "I do hope that poor girl is alright."

"She's probably just visiting relatives or something," I lie.

I don't remember Mary-Kate being on the rose names list, so hopefully she is still above ground and breathing. I head back to Louella and Harry in my bedroom and throw myself dramatically onto the bed.

"Are you ok?" they ask simultaneously.

"No, the Beloved Dentons have kidnapped Mary-Kate and are holding her to ransom for the money we took from them."

"And they told you this in front of your mother?" exclaims Louella.

"They were subtle, but the message was clear – I'll be next to disappear if we don't return the money."

"Are you sure it's them?" asks Harry.

"It has to be the Beloved Dentons because Mary-Kate doesn't have anything to do with the Associates or the Fake-Aidens."

"Do we have to return all of the money?" asks Louella.

"I guess."

"I mean ALL of it, not just what we've got – 'cos how are we going to return Jean's money?" says Louella.

"Well, if they've got Mary-Kate, then she'll be able to tell them about Jean's money," reasons Harry.

"So, should I call the number and just arrange to hand it over?"

"No, not right away – let's just wait a bit and think this thing through…" says Harry.

None of us are keen to return the money to the Beloved Dentons, considering what they have done to those girls. Harry suggests getting them arrested, it could be as simple as giving the police a spade and pointing them in the direction of the rose garden but, at some point, their accounts would be scrutinised and a trail could be made to us. Louella argues that I could claim Denton gifted me the money for sexual services but, I am pretty sure prostitution is illegal and my parents would inevitably find out and even half-a-million pounds wouldn't be worth that happening.

In the end, I make the decision for them – it is after all, my house that they broke into and my mother that they annoyed.

"I'm going to call them and arrange to return the money, we can't risk anything happening to Mary-Kate - or me."

I shake like a leaf as I carefully dial the number on the notepaper. A gruff voice answers and I squeakily respond with my name. The voice asks me if I have any information for them and I am tempted to squeal out, 'take your money and leave me alone' but, I keep my cool, "Just what are you expecting from me?" God, I'm getting slick at this.

The gruff voice sounds annoyed, "Look little girl, we are involved in a serious investigation in which a young woman may or may not be in trouble, so if you have any further information for us that might help with her whereabouts, I suggest you tell me straight up."

"What about the money," I venture.

"Do you know where she got the money from?" he asks.

"No."

"Do you actually have anything for me?" he is getting really angry now and I wonder why he doesn't just come straight out tell me where to bring the money.

I try to push him, "So why exactly are the CID investigating her possible disappearance? Surely it's not the sort of thing you do unless there is a big crime involved?"

"Look kid, I'll be straight with you. Mary-Kate is my cousin's best friend; she's worried about her and I promised to see what we could find out. It's not our usual remit and I could get into a load of trouble for doing this, so please, stop playing games and tell me if you know anything."

"Oh, gosh, I'm really sorry," now I'm confused, "I honestly thought she had gone to Asia after her boss at

Patcham and Co gave her such a big bonus." I cross my fingers and hope I have said the right thing.

"Seriously, he gave her that much money – what did she do, sleep with him?" he sounds horrified.

"I think he was enamoured by her and she really was very good at her job – I think she helped him pull in a massive contract – perhaps that was her reward," I lie with ease.

"Ok, thank you, that helps us understand things a bit better," he genuinely sounds relieved.

"Will you let me know when you find her," I say.

"Yes of course," his voice is so much softer and I wonder if he is possibly in love with her.

I snap my phone shut and rest my head in my hands.

"What the hell was all that about?" asks Louella, sounding as confused as I feel.

"The CID guys were real."

"Do they want the money?" asks Harry.

"No."

I recall the entire conversation to them and they too look confused.

"So they were real CID agents, not after the money?" repeats Louella.

I shrug, "I guess."

"So who the hell was that note from?" asks Harry.

"I have absolutely no idea."

"And where is Mary-Kate?" asks Louella.

I shrug helplessly, again – I have run out of words.

Sisterly Love

Louella and Harry hang out at my house for the rest of the day, I am in an agitated state and Louella has a deeply perplexed expression that is going to cause her serious wrinkles if we don't sort out what's going on and to top it all off, Harry has to go into work later and face his uncle for the first time since learning about his unnatural love of the dead.

My mum has gone shopping with my younger sister and my dad is away on business for the rest of the week.

Malcolm texts, asking if I fancy catching a movie with him but, to be honest, his over-eagerness and lack of experience (and a decent car) are making me reconsider going out with him again. I tell him that I have to help my mum with some decorating this evening.

We watch The Hangover, followed by Meet the Fockers and try to forget about the money in my closet, my missing friend, the perv we killed and cremated, what Harry did to Marjorie, Denton did to Marjorie and most of all, what Uncle Albert does to corpses. We even watch American Pie but, the bit with the apple pie reminds me of Uncle Albert and we have to switch to

School of Rock, which helps – thank goodness for Jack Black.

As Harry heads off to work and my mum and sister return from their gargantuan shopping trip, Louella and I set about making cupcakes, except that mum has run out of frosting so Louella has the genius idea of sticking a marshmallow to the top of each hot cupcake and returning it to the oven until it melts into a sticky, molten frosting-replacement.

"Oooh, they look sooo good," says Francis, "can I have one?"

"No."

"Oh go on, give her one," says Louella.

"No, make your own," my sisterliness has abandoned me today and I am in desperate need of large amounts of cake.

"I'll tell you a secret…" promises Francis.

"Like what? You don't have any secrets worth knowing."

"I'll tell you who put that note under your door."

I drop the cupcake I was about to put in my mouth and Louella nearly chokes on the bite she has already taken.

"Who?" we both squeal.

"God, talk about an over-reaction! Give me a cake," demands Francis.

Louella and I both hold out a cupcake to her and she grabs both.

"Thank you."

"So spill…"

"It was mum."

"Seriously?" I feel ready to pass out with relief.

Francis nods, "She was fed up of asking you for the fifty pounds she gave you five weeks ago, so she thought it would be funny to stick a demand under your door."

Francis saunters off with her reward as I cling onto the counter-top and Louella does the Snoopy-Happy dance behind me.

"Mary-Kate is still missing, don't forget that," I remind her.

And then my phone bleeps with a text from Mary-Kate, telling me that she will be back a week sooner than expected and would I like to meet for a coffee.

After a frantic bout of to-and-fro texting, I learn that Mary-Kate had a duplicate passport after losing, then finding her old one and has been happily frolicking about in Thailand and Hong Kong for the past couple of weeks. She also explains that the handbag the police found must have fallen out of a bag of old clothes and accessories she left out for a charity to collect. I call Mr CID, who is much friendlier this time and I suggest that perhaps he should ask Mary-Kate out to dinner, after which I sit down and eat four cupcakes in a row and wish that mum was out so I could help myself to a calming swig of whiskey.

Louella heads home and I retreat to my bedroom feeling light with relief and sick from too much cake. I sleep fitfully until eight in the morning, when I am woken up by a rough tugging sensation on my right ear.

"Urgh! Charlton, get your stinky fish-breath away from me!"

Charlton slinks to the end of my bed and curls around my feet and I drift into a lovely dream but am woken ten minutes later by the sound of voices below my bedroom window. I yank my feet from under the cat and dart to the window, Charlton barely moves, but opens his eyes just a slither to give one of his seriously-disgruntled-cat glares. The voices are my mother and PC Crink; he is leaning against her car and by the way he is gesticulating, I guess he is asking her about it – I open the window a crack.

"Yes, unfortunately I don't have the car all to myself anymore," says my mother, "and she can't afford to buy her own one."

They continue chatting about the weather, Ed's wife's new job and other boring things I can't be bothered to listen to. I open my wardrobe and pull back my old prom dress to reveal the bag of cash – I really shouldn't leave it in there, my parents could stumble across it but, our house is modern and there really aren't any good hiding places. Ideally, I would drive it to Louella's or Harry's house but, I daren't risk taking anything suspicious looking out of the house when PC Crink and Mr Creepy could be watching.

Then I have a dazzling plan to move the money and to test whether or not PC Crink and Mr Creepy know about the money and are the ones who got that bloke to try to grab it at the coach station.

I phone a courier company and arrange for them to come and collect a parcel to be delivered later that afternoon to Harry's Uncle's crematorium. I load a small cardboard box with books to approximately the same weight as the cash, packing them tightly so that they don't bump around in an un-cash-like fashion.

The courier arrives in a distinctive orange and brown striped van with phone numbers and logos plaster all over it. I take my time opening the door and flirt with the rather attractive, if a little sweaty driver. I can't see them but my ever increasing sleuth's senses tell me that I am being observed. Good. As I head back into the house I hear a car splutter away; Mr Creepy. About ten minutes later, PC Crink gets into his car and drives away too, although he is wearing his uniform so it is possible he is simply heading into work.

At the other end, Harry has been warned to look out for the courier and any other suspicious cars. He is hiding in his van in the Asda car park that backs onto the crematorium. An hour and a half after collection, the courier finally arrives. Harry films it and all the cars that pass by for the next ten minutes after his uncle signs for the package. He calls half an hour later to tell me that a cop car drove by slowly at the time of the delivery, although he couldn't really see who was in the car and that a car like Mr Creepy's had been parked up at the supermarket, opposite his, but the occupant was nowhere to be seen.

Meanwhile, satisfied that both PC Crink and Mr Creepy are occupied, I borrow Mum's car and drive the cash to Louella's ancient and rambling house. As soon as she welcomes me into the hallway, she reaches up and presses on an innocuous looking knot on the picture rail and then slides back a heavy mahogany panel to reveal a sizeable, secret compartment, where we quickly stash the cash, then drive to the shopping centre and spend two hours looking in shop windows, wishing we had had the foresight to bring some of the cash with us.

The next morning I am startled by yet another surprise – the box that I had couriered to the crematorium is sitting, empty on our doorstep. I think we can be certain that Mr Creepy and PC Crink know about the money.

My parents have planned to go away this weekend and my sister is staying with a friend but, for once, I do not want to be in the house on my own, so I arrange to stay over at Louella's house and for the two whole days, I feel completely relaxed.

Then I get a phone call.

Juliette's Reluctant Romeo

-- Louella's Blog: A Passion for Crime --

'Her obsession began with a poster of him, painstakingly torn from a teen magazine. Ten years on, her crush grew to compulsion and each lover had to look like him, smell like him... until finally, she made the right connections, met the right people and was introduced to him. He wasn't attracted to her, but that didn't matter – she had spiked his drink with eight powdered Viagra, locked his wife in a broom cupboard and stolen his hotel key-card. When the Viagra kicked in, he would be forced to retreat to his room, and she would be waiting to receive him – every inch of him.'

-- End of blog post --

"Uh…hello...uh, is that…um the agency that can help with um… uh…bad-people problems?"

Good grief, this is one nervous woman. How the hell has she got my number – and how does she know what we do?

"What kind of a problem do you have?" I try my best to sound like this isn't the first person who has ever called me for help.

"It's my brother – he's got a…a bunny-boiler," she says, as if a kitchen appliance is the sort of problem that we deal with.

"Shouldn't you be calling an electrician for your rabbit cooker?" I suggest - who the hell has a cooker just for rabbits?

"No, no," now she sounds really stressed, "I mean a sexually aggressive and psychopathic woman who is stalking my brother – THAT kind of bunny-boiler, you know, like Glenn Close in Fatal Attraction."

"Oh, I never heard of it."

"How old are you?"

I make a note to check Netflix for Fatal Attraction as soon as possible, "I don't think my age is relevant."

"I need to know you are up to the job, I can't afford to waste money on amateurs playing at solving problems."

Did she just say she was going to pay us?

"Lady, we are certainly not amateurs."

"I…I'm sorry, it's just that I am so worried about my brother, otherwise I would never contact people like you," she simpers.

'People like you', is that how she sees us? I don't know whether to feel proud or pissed and I wonder how much she is going to pay us, I have absolutely no idea what we should be charging, I guess it depends on what we have to do, "Ok, so do you want to tell me a little bit more about your brother's problem?"

"I'd rather meet face to face, so I can explain it fully to you," she says.

No way, for so many reasons. I tell her, "We never meet with our clients; it's a policy that keeps us and you safe."

"Oh, I…I guess that makes sense."

Good. She proceeds to spend the next thirty minutes telling me the life history of her baby brother, until the phone begins to burn my ear.

"Are you NUTS!" Harry is uncharacteristically dramatic, "we only did the last job to raise funds for a dying boy – we had a moral purpose, a good reason."

"Yeah, well, we lost our moral purpose," I sigh.

"Plus, we have three-hundred and fifteen thousand pounds stashed away – that's like…" Louella produces steam as she tries to work the maths.

"One-hundred and five thousand pounds each," I say, "which is enough to buy a small flat each."

"And we've got the cop and Mr Creepy chasing after the money," adds Louella.

"But there is a woman, whose brother is in desperate need of our help – he may even be in a life threatening situation, how can we just ignore them?" I plead.

"That's what the cops are for," argues Harry.

"The bunny-boiler IS a cop, that's why she is so dangerous."

Then I have to explain what a bunny-boiler is to both Harry and Louella.

"What exactly does she want us to do?" asks Louella, sounding like she may be warming to the idea.

"And how much did she say she would pay us?" adds Harry.

"Actually, this job is really simple and she's willing to pay us two thousand for it."

"Where did you get that figure from?" asks Harry.

"Apparently, that's what Mary-Kate said we charged for a simple Surveillance and Evidence Gathering job."

"Oh, an S.E.G. - of course," says Louella sarcastically, "I forgot we had a price list."

"Perhaps we should. Anyway, all we need to do is get photographic or video evidence of this woman harassing the client's brother so they can get a court order against her."

"How do we know where she's going to be?" asks Harry.

"Wherever HE is," I respond, "which is the most exciting aspect of this job."

Harry and Louella look at me expectantly, but I hold out for a few beats longer as this is going to be a bit of a surprise for them.

"HE is going to be in the London tomorrow, attending a film premiere and an exclusive after-party."

"Who is he?" asks Harry.

"Actually, you probably never heard of him, but he writes music and directs videos for most of the pop industry – he's called Romeo Casterlone."

"Don't tell me, his wannabe girlfriend is called Juliette?" jokes Louella.

"Actually, almost," I smirk, "she's called Julia – Sergeant Julia Gott, to be precise."

"A celebrity and a cop," sighs Harry, "Em, I think this is above our level of expertise."

"And too bloody dangerous," adds Louella.

I need to play my winning hand, "Our client will get us tickets to the film premier and the party - which is going to be full of A-list celebrities."

Harry doesn't look terribly impressed but, Louella is nodding emphatically.

"Look, I tell you what - Harry, you can be outside surveillance and video – just like on the Denton job, that way you can ensure mine and Louella's safety and pull us out if anything goes wrong."

Louella is fully on board but Harry is going to need a bit more convincing. Luckily, I have one more piece of information that will clinch the deal.

"Oh, I forgot to mention, Romeo's wife; the poor woman this bunny-boiler is trying to oust is Kylie Jensance."

Harry almost passes out but, at least I know that he is fully on board – Kylie Jensance is his biggest crush; he has all her CDs, posters of her on his bedroom wall and t-shirts from both her sell-out tours.

I tell my parents that I'm staying at Louella's for the next couple of days and we set off to London dressed in our cutest party outfits. Fortunately, Harry's uncle's van has blacked out windows and isn't sign-written, so it pretty much passes as a taxi when he drops us off at the cinema. The pavement is lined with eager fans and we have to fight our way through to the red carpet. I spot the security man our client told us to look out for and give him the code-word. He slips us an envelope containing our tickets and money. Louella nearly swoons at the sight of the gold-embossed, parchment-like tickets, never mind the cash! Goodness knows how she'll hold out when she's surrounded by all the stars of the film.

I have a photo of bunny-boiler Julia on my phone – apparently she usually manages to wangle tickets to wherever Romeo goes. Louella spots her first, already seated inside the cinema, looking decidedly glamourous for a cop. Unfortunately, our seats are nowhere near hers but at least we can see her from where we are.

As I feared, Louella nearly passes out with excitement as the celebrities start piling in and my arm is beginning to bruise where she is poking me to whisper-shout yet another name in my already ringing ear. Thankfully, the film starts and she shuts up; not because she is watching the film but, because probably the hottest guy ever has sat down next to her and keeps running the back of his hand up her bare leg – that is, whenever the woman he came in with isn't looking.

As soon as the film finishes, Julia heads to the queue for the ladies toilet. I jump up too but trip over a stray drink carton and land squarely on Louella's hot seat-neighbour's lap, which is decidedly happy to receive me. He grasps my rear with his clammy hands and hoists me back up, then has the audacity to wink at me! I glower at him and join the queue directly behind Julia, who, to my amazement and horror, turns around and asks me what I thought of the film.

"I…uh, it was great."

"What did you think of the soundtrack?" she asks, "my boyfriend composed it."

Oh good grief, she's deluded, "I loved it, it was incredibly poignant," I gush, "you must be very proud of him?"

"I am," she beams like the proud girlfriend she obviously believes she is.

"It must be cool, having such a talented boyfriend and going to events like this?"

"Oh it is," she laughs, "although to be honest, I don't get to be with him much because he has to do the rounds and talk to all the reporters and media."

Yeah, that and the fact he isn't actually your boyfriend!

The queue takes forever and we end up chatting about all sorts of things – it turns out that bunny-boiler Julia is actually really nice. As we wash our hands, she asks me if I fancy keeping her company at the party afterwards. I'm about to decline, when I see Louella leaving with the groper and his girlfriend.

"Sure, I'd love to."

The party is at a private member's club just a couple of buildings away and as Julia links arms with me I ask if she would introduce me to her boyfriend. I tell her my cousin is a major fan of movie music scores and she would absolutely love a photo of him. Julia agrees but, as the evening passes by, it is clear that she is making excuses not to ask him. For a supposed bunny-boiler, she's decidedly nice and not the violent, scheming woman my client made her out to be. And then, at exactly midnight, she disappears.

I traipse all over the joint, looking for her and Romeo but neither are to be seen and I fear that she has gone psycho and murdered him in some back alley.

I locate Louella, who is cosying up to the groper's girlfriend and quickly extract her; whispering that we may have a situation on our hands. Nervously, we sneak through the kitchens and find an exit to the back alley. My hunches are getting spectacularly accurate.

Well, almost.

Julia is out there with Romeo and whatever they are doing, it definitely appears consensual, as it does for at least three other shameless couples, most of whom Louella recognises. I turn abruptly to leave the sordid scene but Louella reminds me that we need to get photographic evidence, even if it isn't exactly what the client was expecting.

We can't just walk out there and start taking photos but Louella has an idea; one she says she needs a prop for. I look at her quizzically but she just tells me to go back to the party and she'll be back in a while with the evidence we need. I give her my video recording brooch and waste twenty minutes flirting with a super-fit guy who turns out to be gay and flounces off with his equally hot boyfriend - such a pity. My phone rings and I hear a rather breathless Harry asking me just how the hell Louella is managing to shoot the video he is seeing back in his van. To be honest, I really don't want to know. Twenty minutes later, I see her sneak back into the main party room holding hands with both the groper and his girlfriend. All three of them are flushed but Louella gives me the thumbs-up and we leave the club to meet with Harry in his van.

"What the hell were you doing?" Harry asks Louella.

"Having a little bit of fun," giggles Louella.

I think she must be drunk, or high on something.

"You didn't…?" I don't want to accuse her of anything.

"It's fine, I only watched," she reassures me – although I don't really find it reassuring.

"So what about Romeo and Julia?" I ask, "Do you think he's simply having an affair with her and his sister doesn't realise?"

"That's certainly the way it looks" says Louella.

"Well that was easy," says Harry, "we can send the photos to The Client in the morning – no need to give her the disappointing truth at this hour."

I shrug, "We may as well head home – I think our job is here is done, there's really no need to carry on with the SEG."

We head off, passing three police cars and an ambulance with sirens wailing so loudly that I have to block my ears. Thankfully, I sleep all the way back to Louella's house.

Wherefore art thou Romeo?

Apparently, my mobile has been ringing, on silent for the last four hours. The battery is nearly dead and I have to wait for Louella to finish charging her phone before I can finally listen to the stack of messages.

"Oh my god!" exclaims Louella as we listen the final one.

That explains the sirens on our way home. According to our very stressed out client, who probably has a name but, hasn't given it to us, a massive fire broke out in the kitchen of the club last night and now her brother is missing.

"Just how does she expect us to find him?" asks Louella.

I check Sky News on my phone. It mentions the fire but states that the only person injured was a minor celebrity who had fallen asleep inside one of the kitchen cabinets.

"Let's start by finding out where Sergeant Julia is," I say, typing her name into Google, "bingo! She's part of the …oh shit!"

"What?"

"She's in the same police force as Ed Crink."

"Never!"

I show Louella my phone.

"Well hopefully, you won't need to see her again, so Crink won't find out," says Louella.

"I hope so, but, I need to find out where she is."

"Could you call the station and ask if she's there?"

"What if she is, what do I say if she answers the phone?"

"Say you heard about the fire last night and wondered if she was ok?"

Sometimes Louella is actually quite smart. I phone the police station, ask for PC Gott and am told that she is currently busy in an interview. Well, at least we know where she is.

"So what about lover-boy Romeo?" asks Louella.

"I bet he's at her house, handcuffed to the bed, waiting for his kinky lover-cop to come back home," says Louella, looking somewhat wistful.

We phone Harry and get him to search whatever dodgy website he can access to find out her address. An hour and a half later, Harry arrives to tell us that Romeo is exactly where Louella said he would be, but surprisingly, he doesn't look particularly happy about it.

"How on earth did you manage to see him?" asks Louella, "Was he actually tied to the bed?"

"Yes," says Harry, "attached with handcuffs at the top and rope round the ankles."

"Was he naked?"

"No, he was fully clothed."

"Oh."

"You didn't get seen with the ladders, did you?" knowing Julia's connection to PC Crink, I'm feeling more than a little paranoid.

Harry shakes his head and laughs, "Fortunately, she lives in a bungalow."

"Did you take photos?" asks Louella, adding, "for proof."

Harry nods.

"Was he grateful when you rescued him?" I ask.

"I was supposed to rescue him?"

"Well, duh."

I phone The Client back, telling her where Romeo is and about his location and current predicament.

"No, we didn't rescue him – you only requested an S.E.G. If you want a B.R.S. it costs a lot more and takes time to set up, we can't just recover bodies on a whim." I calmly explain.

"No, no…I'm not saying he's dead! No, he's still alive – when I say body, I mean alive or dead."

"Well, who can say – I don't know the woman – do YOU think she's capable of murder?"

I have to move the phone from my ear as The Client has a full-on shrieking, panic attack. Apparently, she does. I wait for her to take a breath and suggest she either call the police or go there and rescue him herself. She tells me she needs a moment and will call me back.

"Shouldn't you have told her that Romeo and Julia are actually having an affair and it is entirely possible that he is trussed up by choice?" says Louella.

"I guess, but Harry said he didn't look particularly happy," I point out.

"Perhaps he was bored of waiting for her to come back and ravish him?" suggests Louella.

The phone rings before I can reply.

"She's offered to pay us ten thousand pounds if we can rescue Romeo immediately," I tell them.

"What if he doesn't want to be rescued – what if he refuses to come with us?" asks Louella.

"He has to," says Harry vehemently, "his wife does not deserve this, so he has to be extracted from Julia's clutches and punished – I mean, HOW anyone could cheat on Kylie Jensance…?"

"Perhaps Kylie is a real pain with bad breath and no bedroom skills," I suggest, but Harry gives me a look that could kill. "Ok, ok, I'm sure Kylie is a lovely, fresh-breathed, porn-star in the bedroom."

This doesn't reconcile Harry,

"How are we going to do this?" asks Louella.

"We'll think of something," says Harry with a Clint Eastwood look of determination.

I shrug as we clamber into Harry's van, then sit in nervous silence all the way to Julia's house. Luckily, there are no cars there, so we hope Julia is still at work.

Harry parks the van in a side street and sneaks through a back alley to the house while Louella and I wait for him to message us. Five minutes later, he returns; out of breath and pale as milk.

"What's the matter?" Louella and I both squeal.

"H..h..his wife!" is all that Harry can say.

Harry appears to be sobbing on Louella's shoulder, which isn't a good look for a young man.

Feeling half brave - half terrified, I tell Louella, "You stay here with Harry, I'm going to take a look."

The three-hundred metres to the back of the house, through a most unattractive and dodgy looking rear access road seems to take forever. I absentmindedly kick a stray can out of my path, then recoil, remembering that I am supposed to be creeping, sleuth-style.

The back gate to Julia's garden is closed, so I open it a crack and peek through. The coast is clear and her garden is a veritable jungle, which means I can easily slip in un-noticed. I avoid the gravel path and sneak between two large fir trees which lead me to a sizeable window. From my position in the trees, I can see two vague shapes moving around inside. I need to get a closer look, so I scoot around the tree to a position away from the window, where the trees don't reflect in the glass.

I spot Julia, pacing around the room; her hands gesturing wildly. Another figure comes into focus; a paunchy male with a mug of tea or something in his hands – he looks just like… Ed bloody Crink! I immediately shrink back, into the security of the evergreens, praying they can't hear my drum-rolling heart. There is a narrow pathway to my right and I drop to my hands and knees to crawl to it, pulling myself upright to peek through the tiny circular window.

The scene is both horrific and puzzling.

Romeo is sitting in an armchair with his head in his hands; his face is a bloody mess and by the way he is cradling his arm, I can only assume it is broken. His wife, Kylie is now tied to the bed and also looking bloodied. This does not make any sense, no wonder poor Harry is in a state. I extract myself and run back to the van, explaining the scene to Louella.

"It seems to me that our Romeo is a bit of a player and now his wife has caught him red-handed and threatened to ruin him, or divorce him, or maybe she is threatening to kill the children in revenge?" Louella suggests.

"And why the hell is Ed Crink there?"

"What do we do about Kylie?" wails Harry.

"Well, I guess we need to rescue them both," I sigh.

We have absolutely no idea what to do and skulk around in the van for a full thirty minutes before Harry exclaims, "Got it!"

"Got what," asks Louella.

"A bit of a plan," he replies.

"A bit of a plan isn't much help," I complain.

"No, but it'll help us if I can get Ed bloody Crink out of the equation," says Harry.

Me and Louella cautiously nod.

"Right, then buckle-up ladies, we need to find Ed's wife."

I direct him to where I am sure Lesley Crink works; a looming, dull-grey office building that looks like the most depressing place on earth to work. Harry asks me what her car looks like. I still have no idea what he plans to do but, we drive round the vicinity of the building until we locate it, parked halfway down a residential street.

"Shit!" says Harry, "this is going to be trickier than I expected."

"What is?" Louella and I ask.

"Removing her wheels," explains Harry, "if we can make her car un-driveable, she's going to have to call her husband to come and pick her up, which gives us a bit of time to get in and rescue Romeo and Kylie."

"What about Julia?" I ask.

Harry shrugs, I guess we will have to think of something when we get there.

It is very nearly five o'clock, which means Harry has to be super quick as well as avoid getting seen by any residents returning home from work.

"Get out of the van you two, walk down to the offices and watch for her coming out – ring me if you see her."

Louella and I hop out and watch from the end of the street as Harry double-parks his van next to Lesley's car, gets out and puts on a high-vis vest and his college lanyard. He then pulls out a clipboard and appears to be taking notes about Lesley's car. If we didn't know he was about to steal her wheels, we would assume he was a legitimate repair-man or vehicle recovery service.

"He's so clever, isn't he?" gushes Louella.

We hurry back down to Lesley's office and sit on the low wall of a building on the opposite side of the road, where we can see, without being seen.

At five past five, we spot her and immediately phone Harry, who tells us he is just about finished. Thirty seconds later, we have followed Lesley to her car and are watching her from behind a pair of extremely whiffy wheelie-bins. We observe her wandering round the tiny, red car; shaking her head in dismay, then making a phone call – hopefully to her husband, then looking angry and making a second phone call. Apparently, the second call was to a work colleague, because a woman who is definitely not Ed Crink, pulls up three minutes later and Lesley gets in. Damn! That plan didn't work.

"So, what do we do now?" I demand of Harry.

"I don't know… maybe we could set her car on fire, that might get him here," suggests Harry.

We all agree that it's not a great idea, so we head back to Julia's and wait in the van until it begins to get dark.

(B.R.S.) Body Recovery Service

Eventually, we spot Ed Crink leaving, so Harry takes the opportunity to creep back through Julia's garden and assess the situation. He texts me and Louella to come and join him and the three of us stand watching and waiting, concealed in the fronds of the overgrown tree.

Then luck turns our way, as Julia grabs a pack of cigarettes from the mantle-piece and heads to the back door. I hold my breath, partly so she won't hear my ragged breathing and because I really don't want to breathe in second-hand smoke.

Harry grabs my hand and tries to mime something to me, but in the depths of the bush, I have no idea what he is trying to say, then without warning, he leaps out of the bush and straight onto Julia, who has her back to us.

Without a thought to my own safety, I follow his lead and help him press Julia to the floor. Louella, who is finally getting the hang of all this, quickly scouts around the garden and locates a length of washing line, which she wraps around Julia's arms and legs. I grab what looks like a dirty old t-shirt from a pile of rubbish and blindfold Julia with it – I really don't want her to know it's me.

Surprisingly, she hasn't screamed, but I guess that would only draw attention from the neighbours, which could then involve her answering some awkward questions about her bound and bloodied bedroom buddies.

"What do we do with her now?" asks Louella.

"We need to question her, find out what happened to make her do THAT to Kylie Jensance," says Harry.

"Should we take her back inside?" asks Louella.

"NO!" I panic, then, remembering to whisper as I don't want her to recognise my voice, "that other cop might come back," I motion to Harry, "get the van – it's dark enough now, we'll put her in it and question her somewhere else."

Harry does as I say and we abandon Julia to rescue Romeo and Kylie. Thankfully, neither of them is secured with the handcuffs and we are able to cut through their ropes with a kitchen knife and lead the bewildered pair through the back garden to the van.

Harry drives as calmly as he can to the rear car park of a derelict block of flats and we turn to face our passengers. Neither Kylie nor Romeo have uttered a word and by the look of them, they have been given some sort of sedative. Julia however, is wriggling with all her might and looks close to breaking out.

Louella frowns at me and begins biting her lip. Harry is scratching his head - none of us knows what to do next. The van is getting too hot and I get out, indicating the others to follow me.

"We could return Romeo to his sister," I suggest, "and Kylie too."

"But he's been having an affair – surely Kylie isn't going to want to be with him?" says Harry.

"But that isn't our problem," I point out.

"Shouldn't we find out what's going on first?" asks Louella.

"I think it's pretty obvious isn't it? I mean, Romeo is shagging Julia, Kylie found out, confronted Julia and Julia got pissed and beat her up."

"I think there's more to it than that," says Louella, "it doesn't really fit that Julia would beat them both up – and besides that, Romeo was tied to the bed BEFORE Kylie got there."

"And what the hell is PC Crink's involvement, if it's just a simple affair?" adds Harry.

Fair point, although I want to get Julia off our hands as soon as possible, so I suggest we interrogate her first.

"The crematorium," says Harry, "I can drive the van straight into the delivery entrance."

"What if your uncle is there again?" I ask, wincing at the memory.

"Nah, he's not been at work this week – picked up some kind of skin infection."

"I wonder where he got that from," I say, sarcastically.

Harry gives me a look – he adores his uncle, despite his icky love-life.

We agree on the crematorium and Harry and I carry Julia in, while Louella herds the other two through several sets of doors to what Harry calls, 'the grieving lounge'. I tighten Julia's ropes and make sure the cover over her eyes is secure, before dragging her over to the other side of the enormous and very plush room. Sitting her down on a rather elegant, wing-backed chair, I instruct Louella to watch the other two while Harry and I start the questions.

Harry will do the asking, with my whispered prompts.

"So, what the hell are you doing to your lover boy and his wife?"

"Who the hell are you?"

"That doesn't matter."

"Yes it does, you are treading on extremely dangerous ground."

"What? We've just rescued two international superstars from your bunny-boiler clutches, what else were you going to do to them after drugging them and beating them up."

"Have them put away for a very long time."

"What?" I shriek, before remembering I am supposed to be whispering the questions to Harry.

"I recognise that voice," says Julia.

Shit.

"EMILY! From the premier, I always remember voices," she says.

"Yeah, well, we needed to get close to you to get your slutty talons off our client's poor baby brother."

Harry shakes his head at me, "Too much information," he mouths, a little too late.

"No, you've got it all wrong," says Julia, "your client is Russian Mafia - her innocent baby brother runs one of the most prolific drug cartels on Earth."

"But he's an internationally-acclaimed song-writer," I counter.

"That's just his cover, so he can travel without causing suspicion, he doesn't actually write anything himself."

I can't believe it, I won't believe it, she's a lying bitch.

Harry gets up and goes over to Romeo with a pen and paper in his hand. He scribbles something on the paper and thrusts it under his nose. Romeo tries to push the paper away with his undamaged hand but Harry is insistent and whatever drug has been administered, it makes him fairly compliant.

"Well, I've finally made productive use of my grade seven piano exam," Harry announces, heading back towards us.

"What did he tell you?" I ask.

"It's not what he told me," says Harry smugly, "it's what he couldn't tell me."

"What?"

"His music skills are really basic – he's definitely not the composer he pretends to be."

"Seriously? But surely someone would have caught him out by now?"

Julia chips in, "That's why he is so reclusive and won't ever give interviews – he doesn't write the music, he has people to do it for him, to create and maintain his cover."

"So next you're going to tell us that Kylie can't really sing," says Harry resignedly.

"Oh, she can sing alright – just like thousands of other girls - she's just had her path to fame made a little smoother with a liberal dose of bribery and blackmail."

Harry sinks down into his chair and covers his eyes with his hands. I think he might actually be about to breakdown and cry.

"Look," says Julia urgently, "you have to untie me and get those two tied up – the drugs are going to wear off soon, then you will have a load of trouble on your hands."

Harry and I look at each other and nod. He unties Julia and passes the rope to me, which I then carry over to Romeo and Kylie.

"We need to get these two tied up," I tell Louella, who looks up from her phone with a completely confused expression.

"I'll explain later, just help me – and quick."

There isn't enough rope from Julia to tie each of them up individually, so we tie them tightly together. Louella glowers as Julia helps us and starts to protest, but I tell her all will be revealed in a moment. Then we sit down and Julia explains the situation in full to all of us.

Apparently, she had been dating Romeo without knowing who he was or that he was married. This came to the attention of Scotland Yard, who then leveraged Julia's relationship with Romeo to get close to other members of the cartel, culminating in a final bust – which we then interrupted.

"So what happens now?" asks Harry, "we don't really want to get involved with the police."

Julia raises her eyebrows, "I think it might be too late for that."

"I'm sure you could keep us out of it," I start – sounding more confident than I feel, "after all, I'm pretty sure some of your methods aren't something the general press would handle well, should the public get to hear about you seducing, then drugging your suspects in order to trap them."

"You're smart," says Julia, "you should consider a career like mine." Then she glances over at Louella, stares at Harry and regards me again, "Exactly HOW old are you lot?"

"Louella and I are eighteen and Harry is nineteen," I confess.

She shakes her head, "Jesus Christ, how on earth did you lot get involved in this?"

Well, I'm not going to tell her the whole story, "We helped a friend get rid of a nasty pervert and they must have talked to someone, who talked to our client."

"What did you do?"

"We hid in our friend's house and scared the perv away when he hid under her bed. He hasn't come back, so I guess we did a good job?"

"Is that all?" asks Julia, suspiciously.

We all nod a little too vehemently and I hope she doesn't probe any further.

"What confuses me," starts Julia, "is why Romeo's sister – Mara, would employ kids to get a cop off her brother's case?"

"She doesn't know how old we were – we never met her and perhaps she didn't know you were a cop?"

"No," says Julia, shaking her head forcefully, "Mara knows EVERYTHING that goes on, she doesn't make mistakes and she wouldn't have employed you without knowing who you were, even if you never knew who she was."

I have an idea – not one I like, because it works on the premise that our client, Mara, used our inexperience to her advantage, "Perhaps, because we are young and inexperienced, she thought we would disrupt what you were doing without stopping to ask any questions – which, embarrassingly, is exactly what we have done."

Julia looks thoughtful and then nods, "Yes that does make sense."

"So what happens now," Louella finally speaks up.

"I'm going to call a colleague to come and collect Kylie and Romeo."

Harry catches my eye, he's thinking the same as me; what if it's Ed Crink?

"What about us?" I ask nervously.

Julia furrows her brow and seems to be at odds with whatever is going on in her brain, then indicates for us to follow her out of the room.

"I should arrest you for assault, trespass and kidnapping… to start with….but…. we all know that it would be advantageous to all of us to imagine this NEVER happened – YOU never happened."

Harry looks worried, "You can't bring more cops here."

Julia looks pensive.

"You can take the van – say you found it," I suggest, but Julia shakes her head.

"I'd have to log it and it would be traced to Harry – questions would be asked."

We all think hard.

"Harry can take them back to your house," I suggest to Julia.

"What if THEY say they've been here?" asks Louella.

Julia shrugs, "I slapped a couple of scopolamine patches on them; they'll do anything you say and remember nothing."

"Is that legal?" I ask.

Julia doesn't respond and I make a note to look up exactly what 'scopolamine' is – purely for reference, of course. So, we bundle Romeo and Kylie back into the van and Harry drives them back to Julia's house, while Louella and I stay at the morgue. We sit tensely until we hear Harry's van return and rush to meet him in the lobby.

"So what now, what do we do?" I ask him franticly.

"Was anyone else there?" asks Louella. I know she means Crink but doesn't want to jinx us by mentioning him by name.

Harry shakes his head confidently, "It's all going to be absolutely fine, don't worry."

"So what next?" asks Louella, "Do we contact our Client and tell her what's going on?"

Both Harry and I shake our heads vigorously, "Don't be an idiot! She knows EXACTLY what's going on – don't you remember what Julia said…we were supposed to get in the way of the police – not help them," Harry explains exasperatedly.

"Do you think we'll be in trouble with her?" asks Louella, biting her lip worriedly.

I look at Harry, he shrugs, "Not much we can do – maybe they'll just realise we messed up and leave it at that – after all, we're just kids."

I don't feel at all confident with his summarisation, but there is little else we can do other than head home.

Captured and Clueless

-- Louella's Blog: A Passion for Crime --

The two young lovers sat, hands and feet bound, awaiting their terrible fate. Finally, the door opened and an older woman entered; model-thin and villainously chic in a red-leather pencil skirt and sadistically sharp stilettos, topped with a crisp-white, authoritarian blouse. He stared at her with a macabre fascination as the woman took a large, jagged knife from her handbag and ran it menacing over the his lover's tongue, leaving a single drop of scarlet blood on her lip. He felt a jolt as the woman bent down and licked it from her, then turned to him, clearly aware of the effect she was having. Unbuttoning her blouse, she pressed against him and whispered breathlessly, "Now, which one of you is going to please me the most?"...

-- End of blog post --

A blast of warm air hits us as we step out of the chilly building, along with two brutish blokes sporting foreign looking moustaches and terrible body-odour. My vision goes as something is placed over my head and my arms are yanked behind my back and held in place by a pair of hands that have probably never seen soap, let alone hand-cream. I begin to yell but one of them whacks me over the head and I sensibly shut-up.

Mine and I assume Louella and Harry's wrists are tied and we are pushed into the back of a vehicle and driven for about twenty minutes before being dragged back out and hauled onto a cold, hard bench.

Our hoods are removed and we all blink furiously in the brightly lit room.

A decidedly diminutive woman paces up and down regarding us. She does not look happy and I assume she is our client, Mara.

"So, what to do with you…" she mutters as she paces.

Another man steps into the room and whispers something to her.

"Shit, this complicates things," she says angrily.

The man exits the room, looking rather relieved to be going and we are left alone with Mara.

"Well, it appears that my darling baby brother and his wife are still in the hands of that bitch cop Julia and now half the county's police are on their way to arrest them. Fortunately, after your spectacular failure, I have other people who can make sure that nothing sticks to them – however, a court case will inevitably mean the loss of Romeo's illustrious music career."

I feel Harry about to say something and I dig my heel into his shin sharply.

"So, the question is; what to do about you three?"

I assume this is a rhetorical question.

"Well? You are supposedly intelligent young people – what should I do with you?"

Apparently it's not a rhetorical question.

Harry ventures a squeaky, "You could let us go – we'll never say a word, I…we promise."

Mara shakes her head and gives a stereotypical villainous laugh, "Of course you wouldn't – especially if I cut out your tongues…"

We all take a sharp intake of breath, but it seems that Mara has watched a few too many superhero movies and is now launching into a villainous monologue.

"…Which of course we are were well known for, back in our hey-day but nowadays, it's just so messy and of course there are such brilliant surgeons who can sew the damn thing back on again." she looks wistful for a moment, "So, the problem I have is that the three of you now know what Romeo is, although you cannot prove anything, and you also know what I look like and that I have unlawfully detained you…"

"KIDNAPPED YOU MEAN!" shrieks Louella.

Both Harry and I elbow her in the ribs and she glowers submissively.

"…yes, kidnapped, if you must…and of course you also know that idiot cop is keeping us up-to-date on everything…"

Harry and Louella raise their eyebrows at me and I shrug then mouth 'Crink?'

"…which means we know who to pay off to ensure our imports clear smoothly through customs, but then we've also got the problem of the bitch cop and my brother's decidedly distasteful desires for her…she'll have to be taken care of… and the idiot cop too, I don't like to keep anyone on my payroll for too long."

Finally, she stops and looks at Harry.

"You have the keys to the crematorium?"

Harry nods.

"And do you know how to operate the cremator?"

He nods again.

She exits the room momentarily, returning with one of her smelly henchmen. He drags us out of the room and down a corridor to a smaller room, which he shoves us into, locking the door behind him as leaves.

Louella bursts into tears and in a wobbly voice asks, "How the hell are we going to get out of this?"

Neither me or Harry answer and I slump onto the floor while Harry peers through the small window in the door, then begins to pace around the room – probably looking for some way to escape. Apparently there is none, as he too then slumps onto the floor in dismay. We don't talk and an hour passes slowly by until the door is unlocked and Mara and her henchmen drag us outside, shove us into the back of a van and take us, well, somewhere.

"Get out quickly," Mara demands as we try to untangle our legs and exit the van we have been bumping and rolling around in for the last ten minutes.

Even before our blindfolds are removed, Harry whispers "The crematorium!"

Shit! This is not good. I am not ready to be roasted.

Mara leads us into the back entrance of the building, using keys that she must have taken from Harry. The henchmen follow, so there is no escaping at this point.

"The cop is going to meet us here," says Mara.

I assume she means Crink, although it's possible she could mean Julia. Either way it doesn't help our situation. I look at Louella, whose head is hanging low like a dejected puppy and I realise that she is not going to be much help in getting us out of here, so it's going to be down to me and Harry to come up with a cunning plan, in the next five minutes, without actually being able to communicate with each other…Nope. We are well and truly screwed.

A mobile rings and a henchman answers it with a gruff, "What?" then turns to Mara and tells her the cop has arrived.

My knees are beginning to go weak as I wonder what the hell we will do if it is Crink.

Bound to be Confused

It isn't Crink, or Julia. It's Mr Creepy.

He's a cop?

He walks in with an air of confidence and the henchmen greet him cordially. Mara actually seems pleased to see him, so I guess he's a thoroughly crooked cop. He glances at us, holding me in his stare for a mere second longer than the others, before turning away and refusing to look in our direction again. He talks in hushed tones to Mara and judging by her wild gesticulations, they are not in agreement.

A few moments later Mara comes back over to us, unshackles Harry's hands and instructs him to light the cremator. Louella looks petrified and I can see she is about to start wailing, so I lean in as close to her as I can to comfort her.

Harry seems to be doing everything as slowly as he possibly can, but he can only delay for so long and soon, a whooshing sound warns me of my impending doom.

The henchman's phone rings again and I hear him tell Mara it's the idiot cop and she tells him to go let him in. This time I am certain it is Crink and I am not wrong. He blubbers his way into the room, looking like he might have stopped by for a pint or two on the way.

Unlike the very cool, calm and collected crooked cop, idiot cop stops dead in front of me and opens his mouth to say something whilst simultaneously pointing viciously towards me – alas, he seems unable to speak at the same time as pointing and Mara has to interpret his mouthing.

"Yes, it's your neighbour; the little slut you like to watch and, I'm pretty sure, get your filthy hands all over?" she doesn't wait for him to respond, "well, it looks like you might just get your wish because I have a rather hot little encounter lined up for the pair of you."

She laughs maniacally at her joke but, judging by the idiot cop's eager looking expression, I don't think he has noticed the burning-hot incinerator yet.

Mara, crooked cop and idiot cop go out of the room and into the corridor where I assume, from scraps of conversation I hear through the thin walls, that they are discussing how to get us into the incinerator with as little fuss as possible.

We HAVE to get out of this.

The henchmen leave the room for a moment and I consider making a run for it, but they return only a moment later carrying loops of rope which they proceed to wind around me, then Louella and last of all

Harry, kind of like you might tie a joint of meat for roasting.

We are propped on the sofa, bound, gagged and without hope.

Mara and the two cops come back into the room. She issues instructions to the henchmen in Russian and they leap into action and grab idiot cop by his arms. He looks completely shocked but puts up a valiant fight, to the point that I actually feel sorry for poor old Crink, but then he is dumped, unconscious, on the floor by our feet and I catch a whiff of his beer-tinged, pungent sweat and hope to goodness they take him away first.

Then Mara's phone rings and she talks hurriedly to the caller, "Yes, wait, I'll come. Yes, I'm sure. Instruct Baylin Crossly, he's the best. Yes, an English lawyer, no, he's working for us – we have his wife - he has no choice… I'll be there in twenty." She shoves the phone back into her pocket and instructs the henchmen to guard the building.

Crooked cop follows her out of the building but, twenty minutes later, we hear a door at the back of the office open and he walks back in. The henchmen are occupied in the office, watching cats on Facebook and don't notice him. My heart begins to try to break out of my chest as I realise that he has probably come back to finish the job.

He reaches out to me first and I gurgle-scream through the gag, trying with all my might to extract one of my limbs from the ropes, but he grabs me firmly and pulls me to standing. If my legs weren't tied together at the knees, I would probably keel over from the stress. He grabs an office chair with wheels and pushes me onto it, then wheels me over to the room with the cremator. I pray that he will knock me out first, but he doesn't.

He looks me in the eye and says in the calmest of voices, "I'm going to remove your gag. You MUST NOT scream."

I nod and I pant in fresh air as he pulls the grubby rag from my mouth.

"Please knock me out before you put me in there," I plead with him, "if you have any kind of compassion."

He shakes his head, "I'm not going to cremate you, I'm going to help you escape, but you have to do exactly what I say – no questions, I'll explain later."

I feel faint with relief and then terrified again as he hands me a small can and tells me to creep to where the henchmen are, break the seal on the can and immediately roll it as quietly as possible into their room, whilst standing as far back from it as possible.

I shake out my stiff limbs and do exactly as he asks – almost getting caught when I drop the can a little too hard on the floor and the henchmen turn to see me dash back down the corridor. Thankfully, they don't follow – whatever is in the can, it works fast.

Mr Creepy has unbound Louella and is in the process of de-gagging Harry when we hear a car pull up outside the rear of the building. I fumble as quickly as I can with Harry's leg rope and manage to loosen it enough for him to shake his legs out of it and we dash to the front, checking first that the coast is clear before legging it into the Asda car park next door.

Mr Creepy points to a large van and breaks into it in seconds. We clamber in and he drives as fast as the traffic will allow for the next forty-five minutes until we reach a wooded area where he pulls the van out of view of the road and finally turns to face us.

"So how the hell did you kids get involved with this?" he demands.

"They asked us to rescue Romeo from a bunny-boiler," explains Harry, somewhat lamely.

"Why?" he asks.

I chip in with, "So, we managed to scare off this high-level perv that was putting the serious creeps on a friend of mine and she recommended me – us to another friend who was having problems with a bloke and… well… I guess good work gets talked about."

He shakes his head, "Fine."

"Is that all you can say…FINE?" Louella shrieks at him, having finally come out of her shocked state, "aren't you going to tell us why you've been spying on us and why you nearly had us cremated?"

"No."

"Are you really a cop?" asks Harry.

He nods.

"A crooked one," adds Louella.

"Are you really going to let them kill Crink?" I venture, "after all, I thought cops stuck together – even crooked ones."

"It's probably too late. I'll have to chalk him up as collateral damage," he says, without a hint of regret.

"So what happens now?" asks Harry.

"I leave, you find your way home and we pretend this never happened."

"I thought you were going to explain what was going on – you said you would back at the crematorium," I argue.

"Get out of the van," is his response.

We don't argue because we are beyond tired, in a state of shock and not even really sure what time of day it is. The crooked cop screeches away and I realise just how bloody cold and hungry I am. We are too tired to talk as we drag ourselves along the road in search of a bus stop. A bus rolls in almost immediately and we scrape together enough cash for the fare to Louella's house.

Fortunately her parents are out and we find what food we can and sink into the sofa, falling asleep in front of the comforting glow of the television.

The Sneaky Shaman

I am the first to wake and find it is ten-thirty, in the morning! The news is on the television, although I barely pay it any attention until a close-up of Julia's face startles me into full alertness.

"Oh my god!" I shriek.

Louella and Harry come to life and glue their eyes to the screen.

"What the…?" starts Louella but I shush her and we listen intently.

According to the newsreader, a massive crime cartel has been disrupted and two major celebrities have been busted as part of the operation – bitch-cop Julia being the woman behind the whole genius operation.

Screen shots show Romeo and Kylie accompanied by a tightly suited bloke, who I assume must be a lawyer and then further news that a cop, thought to be involved with the gang has been found beaten, bound and barely alive in nearby woods. Crink! Did Mr Creepy – the crooked cop, go back and rescue him?

Then a realisation hits me.

"Do you think that Mara and her gang are the Associates?"

"What? The ones your death-by-bed-buddy was running from?" asks Harry.

"The ones who's fifteen grand we stole?" adds Louella.

"It would explain why Crink has been so interested in me."

"It also means that Mr Creepy probably knows too," says Louella, "although we still don't really know if he's really crooked or not."

"Well, we know for a fact that Crink is – and it's damn bloody annoying that he's still alive and breathing," says Harry.

"I think Mr Creepy might be a good cop, deep under cover, otherwise he would have never let us go – or gone back to rescue the idiot cop," I suggest.

"Problem is," says Harry, "if Creepy is good, then we could be in big trouble over Mr Bed and his stash of cash – and if he's bad, then we are still at serious risk of being exterminated by Mara and her gang. It's a lose-lose situation."

"Thanks for that Harry," says Louella, going into full lip-biting mode.

Harry puts a calming hand on her shoulder and she actually looks pleased - I think he might be finally getting somewhere with her.

"It could be worse," I contribute, "we could still have the Dentons and fake-Aiden's parents after us."

"Can you imagine, if they all found us at once?" said Harry, looking somewhat bemused, "The Russians, the perverts, the con-artists and the crooked cops…all after the teen super-sleuths!"

"Oh for goodness sake!" I admonish, "you make it all sound like some kind of comedy."

Louella chips in, "To be honest, it kind of is – I mean, we've got ourselves into a hell of a mess with some seriously dangerous people – and yet here we are, unharmed and in possession of a very large amount of their cash."

"Not to mention some rather sweet narcotics," adds Harry.

We both look at him in confusion.

"The scopolamine – I swiped a couple of Julia's patches, for security."

"Oh great," I sigh, "another thing for the bitch-cop to hold against us."

"So what do we do now?" Louella asks.

The doorbell rings and we all jump out of our skins – guilt, I guess.

Louella peeks through the spy-hole before opening the door to a tall and skinny man, dressed in what appears to be some sort of shamanic robe.

"Aha, the wonderfully-gorgeous Louella, I do hope I'm…"

"They're not here," Louella interrupts mid-gush.

The shaman looks terribly disappointed, to the point that he appears as though he is about to cry, "Oh no! But Sylvie booked her auric sound-bath for today to coincide with the full-moon – I have it written in my diary, see."

He pushes a grubby, bejewelled, purple silk diary under Louella's nose, then suddenly he begins to chant, loudly. Harry and I look at each other in horror until we realise it is just the ring-tone on his mobile phone. He answers with the longest salutation I have ever heard. Apparently Louella's mother is running late and will be there in twenty minutes.

Oh my god, we have to entertain him for twenty minutes!

He flounces into the hall and holds out a limp hand to me and Harry, introducing himself as Paul, then, he practically has a spasm as he announces that he has had the most 'fandabulous idea'.

We are herded into the living room and told to sit on the floor, with our legs out in front of us so that our feet touch in the middle. Paul joins in and we create a four-spoked wheel. He instructs us to close our eyes and place our hands on our bellies and to blow out as much air from our lungs as we can, before all taking a deep breath inwards at the same time.

"Wh-what – the – urgh – ah – hell – is that?" I exclaim, as a tub of the most noxious smoke is wafted under my nose and I begin to feel extremely relaxed, "Oooh, das niiiiice."

Louella and Harry are looking decidedly wonky, although it might be that my eyes are crooked and Paul is prancing around us on his tiptoes.

"That's it," coos Paul, "just relax into it...breath slowly...release all your tensions and with every exhaled breath, name your biggest fear – come on now, don't be shy, no one will laugh."

I bite my lips tightly shut as whatever I have inhaled makes me desperate to talk. Unfortunately, Harry whispers something about sex and a satanic cult. Paul stops his prancing and stares at Harry, but averts his glance to Louella, who is weepily admitting that she is scared that the Russians will cremate her, concerned about how many girls could be buried in the rose garden and really panicking that the crooked cop might come after the massive piles of cash we have hidden in her house. It's all too much and my fear of being found out to be a complete slut slips out through my tooth-indented lips.

Slowly the room seems to straighten out, the smell disappears and Paul is sat back down looking aghast.

"What did you just do to us?" I demand.

"It's, uh it's just a few herbs," says Paul, "they're meant to relax you and let you release anxiety – you know, normal things like being worried about handing in an assignment late, or missing a promotion at work, or being bullied..."

He stops and stares at us quizzically, "What on earth you kids mixed up in?"

I think as quickly as my drugged brain will allow, "Novels – Louella is writing a novel and we've all been busy helping her with the plot – that's what we were meeting here for, to work out the plot."

He does not look convinced.

"You mentioned cash?"

"Yes, all part of the dastardly plot," laughs Louella, somewhat unconvincingly.

"So there isn't any cash?"

Funny how Mr Zen is more interested in cash than Russian murderers and the buried bodies. We really do need to be extremely careful.

"We got the idea from an episode of Murder She Wrote, where a girl had outwitted a bunch of Russian Mafia to steal their stolen money and they were all after her and her friends."

He doesn't look that convinced.

"I don't recall that episode."

"I think it might have been the pilot, which wasn't very good, which is why they only showed it the once," I tell him.

"So how did you see it – you wouldn't have been born when it was first aired?"

I shrug with as much nonchalance as my poor stressed shoulders can manage, "Youtube."

"Oh."

We all turn towards the hall as a key is noisily inserted and the front door creaks open. Sylvie, plus several bags of shopping thrust their way through. Paul jumps up to greet her and we are released from our agonising shaman-sitting duties. Quickly and without a word, we retreat to Louella's bedroom. None of us speaks, we just sit in a dazed – possibly, still ever-so-slightly drugged stupor for about an hour before Harry and I decide that we may as well head home.

People who might want me Dead

I don't contact Louella or Harry for three days and I keep a close eye on the news, which constantly runs stories on both Romeo and Kylie and their previously illustrious careers. Twitter is filled with mourning teens bewailing the harshness of the law and proclaiming their unconditional love for the pair – if only they knew their idols were complete scumbags!

I haven't been able to sleep properly, for fear that there is still someone waiting to get me, so, in my sleep-deprived state, I steal one of my sister's many notebooks and make a list of all the people we have had dealings with, then add their current status:

People who might want to KILL me

Fake-Aiden's parents – being watched and most likely arrested by police.

Mara and gang (The Associates?) – too concerned with trying to bail Romeo and Kylie out of trouble.

The Beloved Dentons – black-mailed into silence and risk of exposure to police.

Death-by-Bed bloke – dust.

Julia / Bitch cop – probably wouldn't risk going after us as we might expose her less than above-board methods.

PC Crink / Idiot cop – currently incapacitated in hospital.

Mr Creepy / Crooked cop – didn't kill us when he had the chance, likely a good guy.

Paul the sneaky shaman - probably nothing to be worried about.

The phone rings just as I finish the list. I am feeling quite a lot safer than before and answer the phone cheerfully. Apparently, I was wrong about my last point on the list. Louella tells me that the Sneaky Shaman popped in for a cup of tea yesterday and she caught him poking around the wood panelling when he was supposedly going to the toilet – he told her he was lost, but he practically lives at her house. We need to keep a close eye on him.

"Do you think it's safe to meet up," I ask, drumming my fingers nervously on the bedside cabinet.

"Well, apart from Paul, I haven't seen anyone hanging around – have you?"

"No, but then I haven't actually set foot outside my house – and barely my bedroom, to tell the truth," I tell Louella, "I could do with some new scenery."

Louella suggests shopping and for once I totally agree that it would be a good thing to do. Harry is working, which is probably a good thing because he always ends up putting ladies underwear in his head when he comes clothes shopping with us, which was funny when he was twelve, but just looks perverted now.

I discover, to my horror that this time, Louella has brought a sizeable wedge of our illicit hoard with her and each time I hand over a note in payment, I fear that it will be flagged up as stolen – which of course is impossible but, it does somewhat add to the thrill of the purchase. Between us, we manage to spend four hundred pounds on clothes and make-up and treat ourselves to the most expensive, fancy coffees we can find. Six hours later, we are done and head back to mine, sneaking our bulging carrier bags up to my room where we spend an hour trying everything on. Shopping is such great therapy! Thoroughly exhausted, we slump on my bed to watch Netflix.

Just as we are dozing off, I hear a commotion on the road outside. Mum yells up the stairs that we ought to take a look outside and we rush to the front bedroom window. Three cars have parked extremely inconsiderately around Mr Creepy's house and I can see several rather muscular men in Kevlar vests sneaking around the side of his house. At least one of them has a gun, or it could be a taser – it's hard to be sure from this angle. Suddenly there are a load of bangs, then shouting and a triumphant looking man comes from round the back of the house with Mr

Creepy in handcuffs. I guess he really was a crooked cop then.

Within minutes they have all left and the street is back to its suburban normalcy. Mum meets us in the hallway looking rather worried, "What do you think that horrid man did?" she asks us, "He always looks so grubby and sneaky – it has to be something really bad, with that many undercover police coming to arrest him."

"Perhaps he's a murderer," I suggest.

"Or a paedophile who likes to watch teenage girls through their bedroom windows," says Louella, giving me a look. I glower back at her.

Mum's face turns white, "Oh god, no, he could have been watching you…." She puts her hand to her face and looks like she might cry, "how awful that someone like that could be living on our street, in amongst poor innocent children!"

A pang of guilt hits me when I realise how far I have travelled from that 'poor innocent child' image my mother has of me, "I'm sure it was nothing like that mum, it was probably just drug dealing or something."

"Louella nods in appeasing agreement, "Yes, I'm sure that must be what it was – he definitely looked like the druggie type."

Mum nods and heads back downstairs. Louella and I go back to my room.

"What do think this means?" she asks.

"I have no idea, but he did save our lives, so he can't be all bad – I think we had better ring Harry and warn him that things are getting interesting."

"INTERSTING!"

"Well, I can't say better, or disastrous, or insignificant because we have no idea why he has been arrested and what this may or may not mean for us," I explain.

"We need to talk to Harry," says Louella.

I agree, but I'm pretty sure mum isn't going to let us out of the house right now, so we agree to meet him at the crematorium tomorrow morning.

Louella stays the night and neither of us sleeps well. We drag ourselves out of the house at ten the next morning and I borrow mum's car.

Walking into the crematorium after our traumatic escape from it the other day is not pleasant, although thankfully there is a cremation taking place when we turn up, so it is full of people – albeit crying, mournful people. Feeling rather inappropriately brightly dressed, we sneak around the back and meet Harry in one of the chiller rooms.

"Why is it so cold in here," complains Louella as we wait for Harry.

"Seriously?" I shake my head and point to a pair of purplish looking toes sticking out from under a white cloth.

"Oh!"

Harry bursts through the door, bringing a blast of warm air with him. Louella flings her arms around him and squeezes him in a tight embrace. Harry beams ecstatically.

We tell him about Mr Creepy and he shakes his head, "But that doesn't make sense. He let us go – if he was truly bad, he would have followed Mara's instructions to cremate us – by going against her and saving us he's put his own life in danger."

"Perhaps he just couldn't stomach killing teenagers?" I suggest.

"I'm sure if he was properly bad, he could cope," says Louella, "I mean, it's not like we're cute kids or babies – I bet even the most hardened criminals think twice when it comes to harming little children."

"What world do you live in?" asks Harry, "have you not seen the news, children are always being abused and murdered."

"She does have a point though, Harry," I say, "a proper criminal would want us gone, so we couldn't talk, they wouldn't risk keeping us around, what with everything we have seen."

"So do we all agree with our initials thoughts, that he must be a good cop, deep under cover?" asks Harry.

Louella and I nod.

"So, what does he know about us? 'Cos if he's a good cop, he's wouldn't like the fact we cleaned up the pervert under my bed, stole his cash, black-mailed a satanic murderer and got ourselves involved with an international drug cartel?"

"I think the only thing he has on us for certain is the fact that we tried to rescue Romeo," says Harry.

"I think he knows about the money and possibly the body we disposed of," says Louella, "although I don't think he has any evidence – and maybe, if he's a good cop, he will just be happy that there is one less criminal on the streets."

Harry and I shrug, it's unlikely but, perhaps Louella is right. Personally, I think Mr Crink is the one we have to worry about, he may be an idiot but, I'm sure he has a good idea of what has been going on. Thank goodness he's still in hospital.

We watch the mourners leave the building and then make our way out too. Harry closes up the building for the day as he doesn't have any more clients and his Uncle is at some conference in Belgium for the week.

We grab a McDonalds and I drive us to the park. We eat in silence, each contemplating the last few weeks. I notice that as we walk back to the car, Louella is holding Harry's hand, I'm pleased for him.

After dropping Harry and Louella back to their homes, I head wearily back to my own home and am shocked to find the road yet again filled with car that don't belong there, with several of them parked in Mr Crink's driveway – oh shit, what now?

As I enter the house, mum comes up to me with a worried look, "Oh dear, oh my goodness, it's so terrible…"

"What?" I demand, getting scared.

"It's Mr Crink – he's dead!"

"Oh thank god!" it accidentally slips out and mum stares at me, open-mouthed, "I mean, oh my god."

She frowns, "Why did you say that?"

"I, um, he was a creep. When you were away he came round here and made lewd suggestions to me and Lou. I didn't like him."

Mum looks absolutely horrified and pulls me to her in a consoling embrace, "Oh my darling, I'm so sorry. What on earth is this street coming to?"

"I don't know mum, but don't worry, I can handle myself."

Mum shakes her head and I extract myself from her arms and escape upstairs to phone Louella and Harry with the good news.

Charity begins at Home

-- Louella's Blog: A Passion for Crime --

She selected the red wig because it suited her pale complexion and in his text messages, he had told her they were his favourite type of girl. She stuffed three hundred pounds into her purse and made her way to the meeting point – he was expensive, but according to reviews, he was worth every penny. By the time Pablo located her in the bar, she was slightly tipsy and ready for anything. Anything except Pablo, who was actually Johan, and an ex-class-mate of her eighteen-year-old son! But then the money was a dead-weight in her bag and the three gin and tonics had loosened her inhibitions...

-- End of blog post --

We meet up again the next day at Louella's house to discuss what to do with the money. I'm all for getting rid of it to a charitable cause, like we were going to in the beginning, but Harry and Louella are keen to keep some of it back for themselves, so we come to an amicable agreement that each of us will take twenty-thousand pounds but, swear not to use the money for at least two years. The rest of it will go anonymously to a local children's charity Louella saw on Facebook;

which partners adult mentors with vulnerable children. Harry agrees to drop a carrier bag of cash to the charity's office.

"What if they have CCTV?"

"Good point Em, perhaps I should sneak there in the middle of the night and leave the bag on the doorstep," says Harry.

Louella and I look at him in horror, "Are you kidding?"

"Ok, maybe not the smartest idea," he concedes, "but how do we get the money to them without them being able to trace it back to us?"

"You could wear a mask," I suggest.

"Unless you're The Man from Uncle, it's not going to look real and they'll probably assume I'm there to rob them."

"I've got an idea," says Louella, "I'll wear my mum's ginger, hippy wig and about twenty layers of clothes to make myself look fat and Em can make me up to look like I've got freckles."

"You'll have to dump the bag of cash on the desk and get out of there quickly, before they start asking you questions," I add.

We agree that this is probably the best plan of action, but just to be on the safe side, I take a pair of latex gloves from under Louella's kitchen sink and put them on before popping to the local Tesco Express to buy –

well, anything really, it's the carrier bag we want to put the money in. I choose a bag of donuts and three bottles of mineral water and carry them back to Louella's. We extract the money from its hiding place and shove it into the bag. Unfortunately, the bags are so thin now that it is blatantly obvious it's stuffed full of cash, so I repeat my shopping trip, but this time to the Sainsbury's Local in the opposite direction and return with a loaf of bread and a jar of gooseberry jam, which was on special offer.

We place the Sainsbury's bag over the Tesco's bag and hold it up to the light. Visually, it seems pretty impenetrable, but the stacks of notes look very much like stacks of notes, so we tear off the paper strips holding them together and throw the cash in loose.

"Can they even get finger prints off carrier bags?" Louella asks.

I shrug, "Probably – better safe than sorry."

"But what about the money, that's got our prints all over it," she points out.

"Yes – and fifty-thousand other people's," says Harry, "plus most notes have drug residue on them too."

We decide there is no time like the present to get rid of the money and put our plan into action.

We need to be quick, not just so Louella doesn't get caught, but also because wearing twenty layers of clothes and a synthetic wig on a warm summer's day is akin to torture and Louella is a drama queen at the best of times.

Harry has his van and he whisks us to the grubby street where the charity has an office in a small flat above a fish and chip shop. We eject a profusely sweating Louella as close to the 'Special Kind of Love' office as we can, without being seen by too many people and Harry and I watch her waddle round the corner and out of sight.

No less than ninety-seconds later we see her running back around the corner, still carrying the bag of cash.

"What happened? Why didn't you give them the money?" asks Harry as Louella pants in the passenger seat.

She looks like she's going to pass out until I whip the wig off her and tug some of the layers loose.

"Paul! Bloody Paul works there – I nearly handed him the money," she exclaims.

"Oh my goodness, he could guess where it came from," says Harry.

"Did he recognise you?" I ask.

"No, when I realised it was him answering the door, I pretended I was looking for a solicitor's office and had got the wrong street."

We all breathe a sigh of relief and Harry drives us and the cash back to Louella's house.

"Well, its proving more difficult to get rid of the cash then it was to get it in the first place," I comment to Louella after Harry has left to go back to work.

"Perhaps we are supposed to keep it all – some kind of mystical forces are stopping us from getting rid of it just yet," says Louella.

"Oh god, you sound like your mum with all that spiritual karma crap."

"I'm just saying that maybe 'Special Kind of Love' wasn't the right charity to give it to."

"Fine, well I'm sure we can find another worthy one to give it to – we just need to work out a safe way to do it," I wearily agree, as we shove the bag back behind the wooden panelling.

To be honest, I'm exhausted from all this stress and actually wondering if I should delay starting university next month and take a relaxing year out. I suggest it to Louella, who is planning to study journalism and surprisingly, she is having similar thoughts.

"I've heard so many people complain that studying writing actually puts them off ever wanting to write again that I keep thinking maybe I should spend a year focussing on my blog and trying to get an agent to take me on," says Louella.

"But do you REALLY want to be known for THAT sort of writing?"

"There's a lot of money in it and I'm good at it," counters Louella, "plus, I've already had a couple of American agents asking me questions on Twitter about my plans for the future."

"Wow, why haven't you told me about that?"

"Um, kind of busy trying not to get cremated, among other trivial things," Louella replies acidly.

I nod distractedly and realise that I've not spoken to Malcolm in a couple of weeks, I tell Louella I'm going home to think about my future, but call Malcolm on the way to see if he fancies a hot date with me.

"Look Emily," Malcolm starts, "I really like you but, I'm not sure you are the right kind of girl for me – there's something a bit weird about you, like your reaction to what your friend's uncle was doing... I don't know, I, er... look I'm sorry."

The phone goes dead and I'm left a little speechless. I'm normally the one to end a relationship and I'm a kind of shocked that he would turn me down. I consider driving to his house and hanging out to see if it's because he's found someone else, but thinking about the amount of people who have been stalking me lately, I don't know if I could stomach it, so I head home and do exactly what I told Louella I was going to do.

Until Harry calls, sounding extremely upset.

A Compromising Position

"Emily! Have you heard – have my parents talked to your parents yet – I guess perhaps not, it's probably not something they'd want to talk about, although but I'm sure my mum will probably tell yours…"

"Tell her what, what's the matter?"

"It's Uncle Albert…you know the conference he went to in Belgium?"

"Yes."

"You know it was a kind of Comic Con for people who deal with the dead for a living?"

"No, I didn't know that," I do wish he'd get to the point!

"Well, it was more than that."

I don't respond, hoping that he'll continue with the story but the pause gets awkward, "So, what was it then?"

"Well, part of it WAS that but, there was also this extra secret event – for people who like to do what my Uncle does."

"Ew! You mean there are lots of them?"

"Hundreds, apparently and they mostly work in funeral parlours or at crematoriums…"

"So anyway, did HE tell you about it?"

"No, the police came round – I was actually shitting myself, thinking they were coming for me, but they weren't, it was because of Albert – they wanted to know what we knew about it, which of course is absolutely nothing."

"How did they find out?"

"Well, apparently one of them was videoing but accidentally live-streamed to his daughter's YouTube makeup tutorial channel. They've all been arrested – my Uncle is stuck in Belgian jail."

"Oh my god, how did your parents take the news?"

"Well actually, my mum took it a lot better than my dad, who's his brother – to be honest, I think my mum might have had an idea how kinky he was but my poor dad has taken it really badly."

"Does this mean you'll have to run the crematorium?"

"I guess so."

"Well, that could prove useful."

"Um, Em, no…I …I don't want to take on any more cases."

"That's a shame, I was considering it for an ex-boyfriend."

"You can't kill someone for dumping you!" shrieks Harry, "Emily, this has all gone too far, and with the police sniffing round my family and probably the crematorium, we've got to keep out of trouble."

"That's a pity," I say, trying not to laugh.

"What's got into you Emily?" Harry sounds really concerned.

"Well, not Malcolm, that's for sure."

"Emily, are you having me on?"

A series of loud giggles confirms 'yes', but I obviously worried him. Perhaps I have crossed the line?

"Look, Harry," I squeeze my cheeks with my non-phone hand in an attempt to stifle any more laughter, "I think it's just the stress of what we've been through, on top of being unceremoniously dumped. I reckon it's probably best if we avoid you at the moment – Louella and I will get rid of the money and we can catch up in a week or so."

Harry agrees and I phone Louella to fill her in on the latest development, but before I can tell her about Uncle Albert, she shrieks down the phone that sneaky shaman Paul might be onto us.

She explains how she stupidly left her mum's red wig on a chair in the kitchen. Paul had wandered downstairs to brew one of his foul smelling, herbal concoctions after a particularly energetic session with her mum and recognised the wig – staring at it, then quizzically at

Louella before stating quite deliberately that it was her mother's favourite dress-up wig and he would recognize it anywhere – apparently he really emphasised the word ANYWHERE.

Louella is now in a complete tizzy about the money wants me to help her get rid of it ASAP. I really don't know what to do with it and, to be quite honest, I can't be bothered to go back around to Louella's again today, so I tell her, I'll come up with a water-tight plan and we will shift the cash tomorrow.

For inspiration, I switch on Netflix and binge-watch eleven episodes of five different crime thrillers, finally getting up to go to bed at three-thirty six in the morning, but as I head out of the lounge, I catch a glint of light coming from Mr Creepy's house.

I sneak to the edge of the window, staying in the shadows so I can't be seen and watch as the front door is opened and three shadowy, male-looking figures walk out and get into a small van that already has someone sitting in the driver's seat. I can't be sure, but by their stature and movement, I am pretty sure one of the men was actually Mr Creepy.

Well, they've gone now, so I go to bed and try to forget about my considerable problems.

Cash and Consequences

I wake up bright and early and with a cunning plan bouncing around my head. We are going to get rid of the cash in a most honourable fashion. I phone Louella and explain my idea to her. She is not as enthusiastic as I assumed she would be but, agrees that it is probably less risky than our previous plan. Harry, on the other hand, thinks it's a great idea and we arrange to meet in town at eleven o'clock that evening.

We are all dressed in black clothing, with no visible brand markings and plain black beanie hats. Me and Louella have tucked our hair under our hats and we are all carrying plain umbrellas – not because it is raining, although it is (thank goodness the British weather can be relied on in that respect), but to shield our faces from any CCTV cameras that we may not be aware of.

Harry leads the way to an area under a narrow railway bridge that is an obvious choice for any homeless person in need of shelter. There are five of them; two are having a drunken conversation about the rising price of local property over a fire in a supermarket trolley and the other three are asleep on piles of newspapers and other rubbish. Louella refuses to go a step closer, holding her nose defiantly. I take a deep breath of clean air before sneaking under the bridge with Harry.

We carefully slip wedges of about four thousand pounds into each of the occupied sleeping bags and the same into the two empty ones, although one of the eagle-eyed drunks spots me and chases us out, yelling and swearing loud enough to wake the dead. The three sleeping-bag occupants don't wake and I keep my fingers crossed they are simply dead-drunk rather than actually dead.

We repeat the same thing in two more locations in town, with Louella opting to act as lookout each time and then head home feeling rather pleased with ourselves. We have managed to get rid of about eighty-thousand pounds and plan to hit two nearby towns over the next two nights to get rid of the rest of it.

The next morning I feel extremely smug when the morning breakfast show newscaster announces 'Local Homeless People Strike the Jackpot!" followed by a lovely story of how one of the lucky recipients will now be able to pay the rent on her flat and consequently get her son back. The newscaster then goes on to completely ruin my day by adding that another four homeless people used their windfall to score copious amounts of narcotics and then sadly died of overdoses.

I guess you win some, you lose some, but I decide against this particular method for disposing of our criminal gains. In fact, at this moment in time, I would quite happily throw the rest of the cash in the river – although with my current luck, it would probably end up on some riverbank to be found by a gang of teenage boys, who would use it to buy alcohol, go drunken joy-riding and likely crash into and kill a well-liked family and at least two elderly war heroes.

I'll let Harry and Louella decide what to do with the rest of the money, then any consequences can be on their heads instead of mine.

When I meet up with him on the way to Louella's, Harry suggests simply moving the cash to a safer hiding place and forgetting about it for a couple of years. I'm inclined to agree with him, but where would we put it.

At the crematorium, in one of the permanent, decorative jars, suggests Louella, who is wearing the tiniest of nightdresses when we arrive at her house. Harry is conspicuously uncomfortable with her miniscule outfit and sits at the far end of the bed, hugging a very large cushion. Fortunately, Harry and I agree with her idea for the cash and she disappears to the bathroom to get dressed, reappearing in barely any more clothing than before, but at least it isn't see-through.

We wait for her mum to leave the house, check to see that Paul isn't sneaking somewhere around, then open the panel to extract the cash.

Except it isn't there.

"Paul!" I shriek.

"But he doesn't know about the secret panel," says Louella, "no one else does."

I raise my eyebrows at her.

"Seriously, NO ONE knows," she reiterates.

"Then who the HELL took the money? A ghost?" shouts Harry.

Louella's bottom lip starts to tremble and her eyes well up.

"Look, if it is Paul, then I don't think we really have anything to worry about – he can't exactly go to the police with a bag of cash that HE just stole from US, can he?" I console Louella.

"But I hadn't taken our share of the money out of it," sobs Louella.

"Shit!" says Harry.

We hear a car door slam and footsteps on the path to the front door. Harry quickly shuts the panel and we try to look casual in the hallway. Louella's mum barely acknowledges us as she rushes in to the kitchen and straight back out the front door.

"That was a bit odd."

"Perhaps she forgot something," says Harry, "my mum is always forgetting things and having to come back for them."

Louella shrugs, "You never quite know where you are with my mum."

I need a cup of tea and head to the kitchen to put the kettle on. There is a letter on the table that I am sure wasn't there before. It is addressed to 'Dearest Louella'.

"Why has mum left a letter for me?" asks Louella, looking concerned as I hand her the note.

She pulls a scrappy piece of paper from the envelope and reads it to herself then with a stunned expression, shakily hands it back to me.

I hold the note so Harry can read it too.

'Dear Louella

Paul has been lucky enough to inherit some money and, as you may or may not know, he and I are quite close. You may also realise that Dad and I have not been in a monogamous relationship for a long time and although I have pretended to embrace this, it is not what I really want.

With his recent windfall, Paul intends to start a holistic juice bar in Thailand. He has asked me to come with him as both his business partner and his spiritual goddess.

I will try to come and visit you and you are welcome to come and visit us.

Much love and blessings,

Mum.'

"Bloody hell! I am sooo sorry Lou," says Harry, pulling her into an embrace.

"That utter bastard!" I shriek, "He's taken our money. How the HELL did he find it?"

I am cross and I want answers. I rush to the front door and look out in the off chance that Louella's mum is still on the driveway, but her car is gone. I slam the door angrily, run into the kitchen, grab a chair and drag it out to the hallway.

"What on earth are you doing Em?" asks Harry as I run my hands along the ornate ceiling coving.

"Well, there is only one way Paul could have seen where we put the money and...THERE it is!" I shout triumphantly as I pull down a button-sized object from a deep crevice.

"A camera!" says Harry, "who put that up?"

"I'll give you three guesses," says Louella.

"But how would Paul know WHERE to put a camera – I mean, that's a lucky guess to put it in the exact spot where the money is hidden," Harry reasons. "I think we need to see if there are any more."

Together, we scour the whole house but find nothing. I'm thoroughly confused – Paul can't have been that lucky to find the exact right spot – Louella's house is massive!

I have had enough excitement for today – my tolerance for drama is wearing thin and I am actually yearning for the boringness of my own family. I get home and jealously watch my sister stressing over homework like it actually matters – if only my life were that mundane again.

My phone rings eight times while I am eating dinner with my family and I ignore it. I need to digest my food before I can take any more drama.

Time to Confess

The confession booth was intimate and she could hear his breathing become laboured and then frantic as she told him all the things she had done and what she had dreamed about him doing to her...

Having let my food digest, I watch ten minutes of inane television before my curiosity gets the better of me and I head up to my room to find out who was calling and discover the missed calls are from Louella with the addition of two voicemails, which I cannot be bothered to listen to.

"What's up? Why are you calling me so urgently?" I moan at her down the phone.

"Why the HELL didn't you answer!" she screams back at me.

"I was eating dinner."

"FINE! Well, while you were calmly stuffing your face, I have had to confess everything to my father."

"EVERYTHING?" my poor heart actually skips a beat and my palms start to sweat.

Louella explains that the spy camera was actually put up by her dad, to watch who came into the house. You see, he suspected her mum of an affair but, wasn't sure who with.

"Isn't that a bit hypocritical, considering he's been seeing other women?"

"I said that but, he swears he hasn't and the only person they both slept with was the sex counsellor."

"He TOLD you that?" I am so thankful my parents are the biggest prudes ever. Suddenly my mind assimilates what she just said, "Hang on....your DAD slept with the sex counsellor too? But he's a bloke?"

"Yeah, I guess my dad swings it both ways," Louella agrees without any kind of surprise in her voice.

"Did you know that he is gay?" I ask.

"He's not, he's bi," says Louella, "besides, that's hardly the issue."

Maybe not for her, but I'm just not used to people's parents behaving like that.

"So what IS the issue?" I ask impatiently.

"He's been videoing the hallway for the past six weeks."

"Oh god. But how on earth did Paul get to see us on the video," I demand.

"He didn't, Dad did."

"So how in heaven's name did Paul manage to find our money?" I ask, feeling really confused.

"He didn't, Dad did."

"Oh. SHIT."

"Precisely," agrees Louella, "and now he wants to talk to all three of us."

"Hang on… so does that mean Paul really did inherit some money?"

"I guess so."

"And you told your dad EVERYTHING?" I ask, "The perv, the fake Aidens, the beloved Dentons, The Associates, Mr Creepy, The Russians, Julia, Crink…. All of them?"

"Yes, and Mary-Kate," adds Louella.

"Has he called the police?"

"No, like I said, he wants to talk to us, all together."

"Did you tell him about Harry's uncle?"

"No, that's hardly relevant."

I suppose it isn't, "What about your mum and Paul – did you tell him about them?"

"Well of course I bloody did – that was the first thing I told him!"

I can't cope with this, I feel like I'm going to pass out, or throw up. I dash into my bathroom and splash cold water onto my face. I have agreed to go to Louella's first thing tomorrow morning. I lie on my bed contemplating my fate until the sun starts to rise and I abandon trying to fall asleep.

I can't eat any breakfast, my stomach is knotted so tightly I can barely breathe and to make matters worse mum needs the car, so I have to get a lift with Harry, who is in an even worse state than I am. Harry asks me if I think Louella's dad will have the police waiting to arrest us when we get there. I tell him to shut up and we drive in uneasy silence.

We arrive to find Louella looking surprisingly calm and a table laid out with tea and biscuits. Her father is serenely sipping a black tea and actually smiles at us as we nervously sit down around the table.

"First of all," he says, clapping his hands together, "I want to congratulate you on your ingenuity and the good deeds you have done for society."

"R..r..really?" stutters Harry.

"Yes," says Norris, "You've potentially saved a lot of people from harm and also done some great deeds – even if they didn't all go quite to plan."

I look at Louella, horrified, "You told him about the homeless people!"

Norris shakes his head, "I put two and two together after I saw you lot take the money from the panel on the night it happened. It is a great shame, but broken people aren't always that simple to mend."

"So, er, what are you going to do with the money?" asks Harry.

"I'm going to put it into one of my savings accounts for two years, until the drama has died down and then I'm going to share it out between you."

"You're going to let us have ALL the money?" asks Louella.

"Yes, you've earned it."

"And you're not going to report us to the police?" I ask.

"Of course not!"

"Aren't you worried the bank will ask questions about the large amount of cash that's suddenly appeared in your account?" asks Harry.

Norris laughs, "No, they won't notice a thing – for one, it's the sort of bank account where questions are never asked and secondly, it really isn't a large sum of money compared to some of my other recent deposits."

"Oh," we all say, simultaneously but, before I can question him any further, he jumps up from the table and announces that we should go out for a nice lunch to celebrate.

I have to pinch myself.

We are ushered into his beat-up Morris minor and driven to a small Italian restaurant about twenty minutes away. From the outside, the place looks completely run-down and inside is not much better, with red-chequered plastic table cloths and decidedly clichéd Chianti bottle candle-holders.

"Does your family come here often?" I whisper to Louella.

"I've never been here before," she whispers back.

We are led to the only vacant table by a young woman with a Polish accent. She takes our drink orders except Louella's dad's, but brings him a drink anyway. I notice that the same thing happens with the food order. Norris nods greetings to at least three of the other tables and as we sit down at our table, he has a brief conversation with a man who could easily be mistaken for The Godfather.

We make small talk while we eat and are each presented with a glass of brandy after the main course. None of us has the appetite for desert, so we leave but, it isn't until we are halfway home that I realise at no point did Norris pay the bill.

Just before we reach home, he tells us that we needn't worry about the Russians or the Associates coming after us anymore. None of us asks why. Louella asks her dad if he has heard anything more from her mum.

"Not yet, but I am expecting her back home within the next week."

"Oh, says Louella, "I thought she had gone for good."

"No, sweetheart," he says, "she'll be back."

"But…"

"No questions, now, I think you two need to go home. Do you need a lift?"

We shake our heads. I climb into Harry's van. He switches off the engine when he stops outside my house.

"What the hell is going on with Louella's dad?"

"I have absolutely no idea," I tell him, although I have a distinct feeling that he might actually be linked to the Italian mob. I think back to some of the strange incidents that occurred at Louella's house when we were kids.

"Do you think he will really give us the money back?"

"Yes."

Shame on the Shaman

Norris was right about his wife returning home within a week, although I am highly suspicious he had a hand in it – knowing what I now, well, sort of think I might know about him.

I didn't find out directly from Louella, in fact, I may have actually found out it was a possibility before her because I happened to be watching the BBC news when the story broke.

'Elusive paedophile, Paul Aruba finally captured during an under-cover operation on the fake charity Police have long suspected was a cover for child-abuse tourism.'

I still feel sick at the thought that we might have given him our money and part of me wishes the police hadn't got to him first. I don't think Harry would have hesitated to light the cremator for this one.

Norris and Louella were interviewed by the police about Paul yesterday, but they genuinely had no involvement or knowledge about him, outside of his sham shamanics. Louella phoned me after the interview to say she saw Julia at the station and nearly fainted, but thankfully Julia merely acknowledged her with a hard stare and left it at that.

I think that means we can safely assume she will not be coming after us.

The only person we still need to worry about is Mr Creepy, who, I am convinced, is hiding out in his own house. I am going to make a surprise visit to him tonight to find out where we stand with him. It's a big risk but, he did save our lives, so I think I should be alright.

I would ask Harry or Louella to come with me but, Harry is exhausted from the stress of running the crematorium single-handed and Louella is terrified the police are trying to find some sort of link between her father and Paul and wants to keep as far away from trouble (aka me,) as possible. So, it looks like I'll be sorting out the Mr Creepy problem alone.

I do wish I hadn't flirted with him at the beginning of the holidays – even if it was only through the window. Oddly though, I don't feel scared - either I am becoming hardened to all this danger or, more likely, the fear won't kick in until I actually confront him. I don black clothing in preparation for sneaking across the road – I don't want the neighbours to spot me, although I doubt Mrs Crink would notice, she's been rather pre-occupied by a number of late-night visits from several of dead Ed's male colleagues.

At precisely three o'clock in the morning, when I am sure no there is no-one else at Mr Creepy's, I sneak out of my house and up to his front door. I consider ringing the doorbell, but I doubt he would answer it, so I creep through the squeaky side-gate and up to the back door.

I try the handle and to my surprise, the door swings open.

Stupidly Brave or Bravely Stupid

'Oh god, I must be mad.'

I take a tentative step into the kitchen, then nerves get the better of me and on the verge of a rather large panic-attack, I turn to run back out, except that a strong hand on my left shoulder pulls me backwards and roughly swings me around to face a woman I haven't seen before. Actually, she is tiny and I look around for the owner of the strong hand who pulled me around. I can't see anyone else and turn to run again, then realise the woman's size belies her ridiculous strength, as this time she grabs me, flips me onto the floor and pins me there with my own arm. I am in shock, but also super impressed.

"How did you DO that?" I squeak.

She smiles and says with pride, "Ex women's judo champion."

"Cool."

I feel her grip loosen and I am able to breathe properly.

"Get up."

I stagger to my feet and shake my arm to bring some blood back into it. She can see that I am not going to try and escape again and directs me through the kitchen to what would be the dining room in our identical house but, in this house it seems to be set up as some sort of video monitoring centre, with Mr Creepy sitting in a plush leather chair in the middle of it all.

"What the hell are YOU doing here," he snarls.

I take a deep breath, I'm not going to be intimidated by him, "I want answers," I tell him.

"Answers to what, specifically?"

"Everything - starting with why you let us go."

"A sensible kid would be happy to be alive and leave it at that."

"I'm not a sensible kid," I snap back, wondering how long my display of over-confidence can last.

"Sit down," he commands.

"What on?"

He tells the woman to bring a chair in and I gratefully sit down before my legs give way.

"Before I tell you anything, I need a little security," he says, leaning within a hand's width of my face.

The blood drains from my face and I wonder what the hell he is going to ask for. I don't answer and simply stare, stony-faced, eye-to-eye with him. I know he is trying to break me down but I am stronger than he thinks – although evidently not as strong as his partner, who places her hand on my neck and inflicts more pain with her thumb than I would have ever thought possible, especially with such cutely manicured nails.

Unfortunately, my face gives way to a wince and Mr Creepy can see I am not unbreakable. He smiles and nods to the tiny Hercules to let go.

"Just so you understand, we have no qualms about inflicting pain on you, should you become a problem," he says.

I nod compliantly.

"And you will become a problem once you know what we are doing, which is why I need you to understand the gravity of what you getting involved in."

"I get it, you'll hurt me if I tell anyone," I say, getting rather bored of the dramatic lead-up.

"And," he pauses, "I want to know what YOU have been up to first."

"Could you please specify," I ask him, knowing that there is very little chance that he actually does know everything.

He shakes his head and laughs, "You've got good at this, but the problem is, if I tell you what I know about you, I might miss out on the bits I don't know however, if you don't know what I do or don't know, then you are more likely to tell me things I don't already know about."

"Uh, I guess."

"So…."

"Where shall I start?" I'm hoping he'll at least give me an idea of when he became aware of our crime-busting operations.

"From the beginning," he says, "when you killed, cremated and stole from one of my most valuable assets."

Oh crap, "Am I going to go to jail?" I squeak, having entirely lost my bravado.

He shakes his head and looks at Tiny Hercules, who nods as if giving permission for something.

"If you have done everything I believe you have done, then you are actually of great value to someone like me – I could utilise you."

"By utilise, do you mean employ?" I have to be clear, because utilise could have nasty connotations.

"Yes."

I breathe a sigh of relief, "Ok."

For the next hour, I am mentally probed about every aspect of my life over the summer holidays. He even wants to know if I ever actually slept with Malcolm and how far I went with Louella – I'm not sure this information is necessary but, he seems very keen to get it all down in his little notebook.

"Why are you writing this down by hand?" I ask, when he finally puts his pen down to rest.

"You really do think about every detail, don't you?" he answers.

"I have an inquisitive mind – so, why pen and paper instead of the computer?"

"Because this information is only for me."

Well, that's a relief, I think.

"So, let me tell you a little bit about my operation," he finally says.

He explains that although Mara and her gang of Russians appear to be the big fish in the media, they are in fact the 'smoke and mirrors' for a much larger operation involving global corruption at government level over several continents. He doesn't specify which ones but, he does say that the operation is so secret that there are only a handful of operatives working on it and they are all using the cover of other large operations. To be perfectly honest, it's all rather boring and not at all James Bond.

"So, will you consider joining our programme?"

"Huh? What?" I must admit I zoned out a little bit and didn't quite catch the last bit.

He repeats, "Would you like to join our programme as a trainee operative?"

Oh my goodness! Is he asking me to become an international government agent?

"Hold on a moment," I stall as I gather my thoughts, "you are asking me if I want to join your organisation?"

He nods.

"Is this based on me breaking in here tonight or were you going to ask me anyway?"

"It was something we had already discussed, but your breaking in here confirms our suspicions about your potential."

"And what about the others – Louella and Harry?"

"Your girlfriend is of no use to us," the tiny Hercules shrugs dramatically, "there is a conflict of interest."

I nod, "Norris."

Tiny Hercules narrows her eyes at me and I mime a zip across my mouth, which she does raise a slight smile at.

"And Harry…?"

"Ah, yes – the boy," Mr Creepy grins, which almost makes him look handsome and I realise, through the meagre light, that he is not dressed in his usual grubby-looking clothes, and his hair is actually washed and styled. I feel marginally better about having flirted with him.

He continues, "It would appear that he will be running his Uncle's crematorium for the foreseeable future, which could prove useful in our line of work – couldn't it?" He looks at me with raised eye-brows.

Without a shred of guilt, I respond, "Yes, it most certainly could."

Mr Creepy nods.

A screen suddenly flickers violently behind him and a disembodied voice reels off some sort of code.

"Time for you to go now, Natalie will see you out."

Mr Creepy turns to his screens and I am taken to the door.

Natalie smiles at me, "You did well in there, we will be in touch."

I sneak across the road and back into my bedroom and fall promptly asleep.

All Tied Up

I told Mum that I now planned to take a year out before starting university. Mum suggested volunteer work in a third world country, but I said that having watched some videos online, I realised there was a distinct lack of sanitation in most of the countries on offer, so I got myself a job assisting in a school in Utah. The bit about Utah is true but the school I am going to is definitely not for kids and not listed on any map.

Louella flew out to LA three days ago, on an invitation to see someone important in publishing, she says. I hope it's the publishing deal she dreams of, but I'm worried it's more likely to be something to do with the porn industry, bearing in mind the stuff she's written. Oh well, that would probably suit her just fine anyhow.

Harry is already pining after her and I really hope she comes back, but he's got enough on his plate trying to run the crematorium.

11479528R00118

Printed in Germany
by Amazon Distribution
GmbH, Leipzig